I0585423

VISIONER

THE SHIFTER WAR BOOK TWO

K K NESS

Copyright © 2017 K K Ness.

All rights reserved.

www.kkness.com

This is a work of fiction. Names, characters, places and incidents are the product of the author's imagination, and any resemblance to actual events, organizations, businesses, locales or persons, living or dead, is entirely coincidental.

Unauthorized reproduction or distribution of this copyrighted work is illegal. No part of this book may be reproduced, loaned or used without written permission, except where permitted by law. To request permission and all other inquiries, contact the author at the website above.

Cover art by Deranged Doctor Design

ACKNOWLEDGEMENTS

For Ma.

We acknowledge the Bindal and Wulgurukaba people upon whose Country this book was written.

Danil pushed through the ferns, his homespun tunic damp with cold as a slow drizzle swept down from the Amasian mountains.

A stream led him east, where trees grew thick and wild. Danil could hear the steady drip of water echo deep within long abandoned mine shafts as he passed their entrances. He took care to step clear of the unstable shale fields covered with newly grown moss and lichen as a force he didn't understand, but was compelled to follow, drew him forward.

An abandoned hut emerged from the early morning gloom, its door askew and mud walls overrun with vines. More huts sat amongst the sprawling trees and thick undergrowth, marking where the village of Farin and its people had once eked out a harsh existence on the edge of the deadlands. Danil paused at a blackened mound, bile rushing into his mouth as he was assaulted with memories of what lay beneath.

He could never forgive the magi of Roldaer for what they had done in their quest to awaken the halfbreed, Kaul.

The promise of kiandrite crystals, the source of the magi's waning power, had seen the Roldaerians cut a path of destruction through everything Danil had once held dear and forced him to become a traitor to his people to prevent a catastrophic war. In the process, Danil had discovered a connection to the deadlands not seen since the Great War, and his life irrevocably changed.

Danil felt a soft hum beneath his feet, a gentle whisper of comfort wrapping itself around his mind. As he watched, a single flower pushed its way through the blackened soil. Petals of shimmering blue peeled open as though to embrace the awakening day. Balance was returning.

Breath pluming, Danil continued deeper into Farin as a force that had been calling him for days beckoned him closer. He paused in the town square, recalling better times when a troupe of acrobats had performed, and the once vibrant streets had been filled with laughter. Instinctively, Danil crouched beside a ring of mushrooms and pressed a hand to the wet soil. A soft murmuring filled his mind as magic pushed up through the ground. He waited.

There, burrowing its way out of the dark mud, was a kiandrite crystal. No larger than his forefinger, it changed from silver to blue as Danil gently wiped away the remaining dirt. The Corros House glyph on his palm glowed as if in greeting, and he felt a surge of warmth when the crystal momentarily turned gold to match.

An oversized red wolf trotted out from the undergrowth and padded toward Danil with a confident swagger. Danil buried his hand in the fur before scrunching his nose as the wolf snuffled happily in his face. The wolf gave him a grin, tongue lolling to one side in amusement. Spying the crystal, the wolf tilted his head curiously and nosed at it. The air shimmered, and suddenly Hafryn crouched beside him, green eyes reverent.

"Your first crystal as custodian, Danil," he murmured in awe.

Turning it about to catch the weak morning light, Danil said, "It's beautiful."

The heart of the crystal brightened to emerald.

Hafryn snorted. "It knows it has admirers."

Danil grinned. "I guess so. Though I didn't expect to find it in Farin." An old ache settled in his throat as he glanced once more at the decaying buildings around them.

The wolf shifter shrugged. "You grew up here, no? Perhaps it chose this place in honor of your custodianship."

Danil supposed Hafryn had a point. Only two months had passed since the failed magi plot. It was his duty now to ensure that the magic that had been trapped for centuries by Kaul's desire for domination was able to grow across the land as originally intended.

"Should I keep it?" Danil asked. The crystal sent a warm, buzzing vibration up his arm.

"It would be an insult not to, *fala*. We can't leave it here, in any case. Roldaer isn't the best place for kiandrite."

Danil grunted. Any magi who came upon the crystal would grind it up for spells and curses. "We shouldn't be here in any case—Elania and Blutark won't like that we've left the deadlands."

Hafryn winked. "Your tutors are probably wondering why you've skipped out on a lesson."

Groaning, Danil said, "As long as they don't make me create magelights, I'll do double."

"Magelights aren't so difficult."

"For Amasians, maybe," Danil groused. Most days, even the simplest enchantments seemed beyond his ability to master. Magelights were one of the enchantments taught to younglings just coming into their gifts. He eyed Hafryn. "I've never seen you make one."

Hafryn rose to his feet and stretched his arms above his head to expose his lithe belly. "I have other talents."

"I'm aware," Danil replied dryly.

Hafryn's grin turned rakish as he gripped the fabric of Danil's tunic. Danil let himself be tugged up and close until the full length of his body pressed against Hafryn's. The shifter's green eyes brightened. "I suppose you are, *fala*."

Suddenly, the crystal in Danil's hand burned angrily, and he stepped away from Hafryn in alarm. "Why is it—?" Danil stopped at the crunch of footsteps in the leaf mold.

They whirled as six Roldaerian soldiers stepped out from behind the fernery. Swords drawn, they crowded close.

The crystal in Danil's fist darkened.

Air rippling, Hafryn transformed back into a snarling wolf. He pushed in front of Danil, hackles bristling as he bared his teeth. Danil gripped his ruff and buried the crystal in his pocket. Hastily he drew the dagger at his waist. Beneath him, the leylines stirred in agitation.

A middle-aged woman stepped between the soldiers. Finely dressed in red robes and fur-lined cloak, she bore an officious silver crest on a long chain about her neck. Her pale hair was held back by a jeweled clasp, her dark eyes mild as they swept over Danil and Hafryn.

"How momentous to find you here," she said, drawing closer. Her robes rustled over ferns and detritus.

Hafryn's growl deepened. He pushed back into Danil's legs, propelling him away from the Roldearians.

Pausing, the woman pressed a hand to her chest. "Oh, there's no need for alarm, Amasian," she said, eyes wide. "I bring you no ill will."

Danil eyed her and the soldiers critically. "Then why are you here?"

She curtseyed, making the jewel in her hair twinkle. "I am Arlyn Nera, an emissary of King Liam of Roldaer." Straightening, she smiled. "I have been tasked to make contact with the High Council of Amas. We wish to parlay for peace."

2

Against his better judgment, Danil led the emissary and two of her soldiers into the deadlands.

They stuck to groves where ferns and trees grew thick, the streams running clear of the remnant foulness still leaching into other parts of the deadlands not yet touched by the leylines. Hafryn strode beside him in wolf form, his shoulder brushing against the back of Danil's leg. A low growl of warning emitted from his throat whenever the soldiers stepped too close.

The leylines themselves thrummed with energy beneath Danil's boots.

"Fascinating," Arlyn marveled as she drew up beside Danil. She pointed to the rich canopy with its epiphytes and hanging moss. "I expected the deadlands to be nothing but rocks and poisoned water. How, pray tell, did this come about?" Her eyes were bright with wonder.

"Ask Magus Brianna," Danil muttered as he ducked under a low branch.

The Roldaerian emissary smiled. "I'm afraid I never met her, and my sources inform me that her memory of what transpired here is lost." She eyed him speculatively. "I did receive missives regarding you, though, Danil of Farin. Your Roldaerian accent is unmistakable."

Danil paused, staring. "I'm sure whatever you read was enlightening, Emissary Arlyn."

"Please, just Arlyn," she said with another warm smile. "I believe we want similar things, Danil."

"How do you figure that?" He continued along the banks of a stream. A small school of fish scattered when his shadow swept over them.

She gave an elegant shrug and held her hand out to him for help to cross the stream. Begrudgingly, Danil offered her his arm. "War is hardly to our kingdom's benefit, Danil," she said. "I'm certain it's the same for Amas."

"It's not Amas who invaded Roldaer," Danil pointed out. "Magus Brianna sent a contingent into Altonas to steal kiandrite and relics."

"A misdeed I hope to address," Arlyn said, her voice determined. "But we didn't just now come upon you and your wolf in neutral territory, either, Danil."

Danil frowned. "Farin was my home until Magus Brianna murdered everyone in it."

"A terrible offense on her part," Arlyn murmured, her expression sympathetic as she patted his arm. "But the village nonetheless remains part of Roldaer, and no Amasian should be there." She tightened her grip on his arm and pulled him to a stop. Her eyes glowed earnestly. "Danil, you must know that I mean no ill will. I want peace between us. I wish merely to point out that both sides have made mistakes."

"Mistakes," Danil repeated, a little astonished at how she measured different transgressions.

She smiled and tilted her head coyly. "Of course. But I'll

fuss over it no more. I won't even demand that you return that mage-crystal you stole from Farin."

Danil resisted the urge to touch his side. The crystal was a warm hum in the back of his mind. "A generous gesture, Arlyn," he gritted out.

The emissary beamed. "Think nothing of it. We are going to be firm friends, you and I."

Hafryn snapped the air angrily with his teeth. Abruptly he trotted ahead to where the stream forked around a large boulder. A familiar voice called out, and suddenly Blutark emerged with his bow in hand. Easily a head taller than Danil, Blutark was an imposing figure even in his human form. He took a bead on Arlyn, the glyphs on the arrow's shaft glowing.

"Step away, Roldaerian," Blutark growled.

Hafryn transformed and made a quelling gesture. "We're escorting Emissary Arlyn to camp."

Arlyn raised her hands, smiling. "Enchanter," she said to Blutark. "Forgive our unannounced arrival."

Eyes narrowing, Blutark lowered his bow but kept the bowstring taut. "You'll honor peace in the camp, Roldaerian?"

"Of course."

Blutark motioned to the two soldiers flanking Arlyn with his chin. "How many more in your retinue, emissary?"

"Four, but they are content to await my return in Farin."

Blutark nodded, but Danil could tell by the tightness around the bear shifter's mouth that he wasn't ready to believe her. He motioned Danil to him. "Lead the way, Danil."

A graveled path led them out of the grove and onto a barren expanse of exposed rock. A snow leopard sat waiting for them, amber eyes watchful. Her tail flicked as the Roldaerian soldiers passed. She shared a meaningful look with Blutark before falling in behind them.

They reached the camp in time for an immense golden dragon to wheel overhead.

Dust swirled and eddied beneath the stroke of mighty wings as the dragon landed upon the rocky plateau to the west of the camp. Shielding his eyes, Danil waited as the dragon folded his wings and transformed into a tall, dark-haired man. A sword sat at the dragon shifter's hip, his shirt brocaded with gold, his boots polished to gleaming. A sapphire ring flashed in the sunlight.

"Sonnen," Hafryn said, striding across to clasp the man's arm heartily.

The dragon prince's eyes turned foreboding when they landed on the Roldaerians. "What has happened?"

Arlyn curtseyed, while the two soldiers behind her bowed. "Prince Sonnen, I am Emissary Arlyn Nera. My king has tasked me to negotiate with the High Council of Amas for peace between our great kingdoms."

Golden eyes unreadable, Sonnen inclined his head. "Emissary Arlyn, this is an unexpected pleasure. Blutark, please organize refreshments for the emissary and her escort."

Arlyn smiled and curtseyed again. "Your generosity is appreciated, Your Highness. I hope you can join me when it suits. We have much to discuss."

Sonnen gave her a terse nod.

She and her soldiers followed Blutark down into the camp. Elania, still in her snow leopard Trueform, padded silently up to Sonnen. She gave a questioning chirrup.

Flames showed in Sonnen's eyes as he watched the

Roldaerians enter one of the brightly colored tents lining the gully below. Pennants with the glyph of Corros snapped and furled in the breeze above the camp.

"Elania," Sonnen rumbled. "Take a contingent east. We must know how many Roldaerians are at the border."

"Emissary Arlyn says there are just four," Hafryn said.

"Do you believe her?" Sonnen asked.

"Of course not."

Sonnen returned his gaze to Elania. "Find where they are, but do not engage. Report back to me by nightfall."

Elania gave a small warble of agreement and took off at a lope down into the camp.

Sonnen turned to Hafryn and Danil. "What fresh game is this?"

Hafryn shook his head. "I'm certain I have no idea. But the emissary is well informed. She knew Danil just by his accent, and Blutark, too."

"Then it is fortuitous I returned early," the dragon prince said. "The High Council has adjourned to contemplate our course of action against Roldaer."

Hafryn studied his friend. "Can we expect things to go our way?"

Sonnen's mouth tightened. "The councilors are unconvinced that protecting the deadlands is an Amasian problem. Emissary Arlyn may prove a boon to them."

Danil's shoulders sank. The deadlands had been left to languish for centuries as a desolate buffer between Amas and Roldaer. It was only after the leylines had been freed that life began to thrive once more in the gullies and canyons. As custodian, it was Danil's responsibility to protect the leylines from being plundered for their magic. He had little idea how to succeed without Amasian aid.

Sonnen turned to Danil, his eyes assessing. "The High

Council would do well do visit here. You've been busy, custodian. The greening of the deadlands continues apace —an impressive sight from the air."

Danil shrugged, forcing down a flare of pride. "It's all the leylines' doing."

Sonnen swept his hand toward the ferns and saplings marking the path down into the camp. "You underestimate your achievements, Danil. The leylines have done well under your guidance."

Such praise only caused a knot in his belly. "The High Council doesn't seem to care what happens if the leylines are lost to Roldaer."

"It will be a generation at least until there is harvestable kiandrite," Sonnen muttered in agreement. "Time enough for the deadlands to be someone else's problem."

Hafryn gave the dragon a chagrined look. "About that..."

Sonnen frowned. "The first crystal has emerged? It is too soon, Hafryn."

"I sensed it three days ago," Danil said, recalling the warm buzz that had pulled him from sleep. "We found the crystal in Farin."

Sonnen grimaced. "That is unfortunate."

Hafryn gave Danil a comforting look. "But it also makes sense, considering Danil's heritage."

"Aye." The dragon prince rubbed his face. "However, no kiandrite has been harvested in Roldaer for centuries. Some councilors will see today as a bad omen, no matter that a first crystal is always cause for celebration."

Heart heavy, Danil said, "It's my fault. I'm supposed to herd the leylines into safe groves, not into Roldaer."

"You are the reason the leylines exist at all," Sonnen countered, voice firm. "Do not forget that, custodian."

Danil managed a nod but feared that his inability to

control the leylines would allow the magi to return to power. The thought of their dark magic being powered by the kiandrite that he was supposed to protect made him feel ill.

"May I see it?" Sonnen asked.

Blinking, Danil took the small crystal from his pocket. It turned sullen yellow at being handed over.

Sonnen lifted it toward the weak sunlight streaming through the clouds. "A handsome stone," he murmured. The crystal momentarily flickered blue before returning to yellow. "And its heart belongs to you, Danil. You should keep it close."

The dragon wove a symbol in the air. Long silver twine came into being to wrap around the crystal. Sonnen handed it back, and Danil tied the cord about his neck. The gem swirled blue and purple against his chest.

"Thank you," Danil said.

"For now, its origins should remain hidden," Sonnen declared. "We have allies on the council, but the Houses far removed from the border are slow to understand the danger we face. Let's not give them any reason to doubt our cause, or your loyalty, Danil."

"Danil has proved his loyalty, Sonnen, many times over," Hafryn growled.

"I agree," Sonnen said. "But there are those who will think otherwise. That discussion is for another time, however." He motioned toward the graveled path leading down into the camp. "Let us see what terms the Roldaerian emissary has to offer."

They passed under twin pennants that marked the entrance to the camp. Sturdy wooden walkways threaded between ferns and the stream that disappeared into a disused mine shaft at the far end of the gully. A handful of shifters called out in greeting as they headed for the main tent, where the scent of spiced tea was thick and welcoming.

Sonnen motioned for the tent flap to close behind them before taking a seat amid the plush, embroidered cushions. Emissary Arlyn was already perched on a bright orange pillow, taking dainty sips from her cup. Her two soldiers stood to attention behind her. Danil and Hafryn took up similar positions behind Sonnen, while Blutark stood by the brazier, arms folded over his imposing chest.

Arlyn watched them all over the rim of her cup.

"Emissary Arlyn." Sonnen poured himself a steaming cup and settled back. "I trust this tent is suitable for our discussions."

"It will serve, Your Highness," Arlyn nodded politely.

"You wish to consider terms."

Arlyn smiled and set down her cup. "You are to the point, Your Highness. I like that." She folded her hands in her lap. "Very well. It is the wish of King Liam of Roldaer that our two kingdoms return to diplomatic talks for settling our quarrel."

Sonnen studied her. "Which quarrel do you refer to, emissary? By my reckoning, there is the recent issue of invasion, murder, and thievery by your magi and their soldiers. Not to mention the continued abduction of our people."

Arlyn nodded, momentary steel in her eyes. "These are among the matters I must bring before the High Council, Your Highness."

Sonnen cocked a brow.

Arlyn smiled again. "Forgive me, Prince Sonnen. I am merely following the dictates of my king."

"The High Council is not here."

"That's unfortunate, but not unexpected. If the High

Council is unable to come to neutral territory, then I am amenable to traveling wherever you deem suitable."

"You are." Sonnen raised an eyebrow in surprise.

Arlyn matched his expression. "Naturally. For the good of both our kingdoms, Your Highness."

3

Late afternoon saw Danil treading the shadowed path to the far end of the gully. The rush of water took him to the mouth of an abandoned mine shaft, where the stream disappeared into the darkness with a dull, frothy roar.

Danil settled on a boulder overlooking the mine shaft. The pad of animal feet behind him indicated that at least two Amasians slinked in the undergrowth to keep watch. He nodded his thanks. The arrival of the Roldaerians had set the whole camp on edge.

With a sigh, Danil unrolled a sheaf of parchment and set it upon the boulder together with a stick of charcoal. Taking hold of the crystal at his chest, Danil closed his eyes and searched for the meditative state he so often reached while training with Elania and Blutark. The shimmering gem was a low murmur in the back of his mind. Beyond, the leylines felt like iridescent bursts of color as they stretched through cracks and fissures in the rocks. The thrum of verdant shoots and awakening seeds spread out across the deadlands.

Danil's fingers found the charcoal. He sketched

passively, letting his connection to the kiandrite and leylines dictate the shapes on the parchment. Whispers seemed to rise above the roar of the water, and half-formed images played across his vision.

Eventually, he looked down. The parchment was a mess of scrawled lines and swirls, looking nothing like any of the glyphs he'd seen during his time with the Amasians.

Danil slumped in disappointment and noticed Hafryn's approach from the wooden boardwalk.

The wolf shifter had a smooth, predatory gait, his hand naturally gravitating to the hilt of his sword. His braided hair appeared fire-red in the dappled light, and he grinned when he noticed Danil watching him.

Blushing, Danil rose to his feet. "I thought you'd still be with Sonnen."

Hafryn offered a hand to help him down from the boulder. "Elania's returned. The emissary told the truth—there's only the soldiers we came upon this morning."

"You sound disappointed," Danil said as he gathered the charcoal and parchment.

Hafryn said, "I don't trust Arlyn. It would have been convenient to have proof." He considered Danil. "What have you been up to?"

"It's nothing," Danil replied quickly.

Hafryn merely waited, green eyes patient.

Danil leaned against the boulder and handed Hafryn the parchment with a sigh. "I'd hoped to create a glyph," he admitted. "Something to protect the leylines now that Roldaerians are here."

"You don't trust Arlyn either."

"How can I? She's a representative of King Liam, and we both know what he allowed to happen in Farin."

Hafryn eyed the parchment. "I don't think even

custodians can create glyphs, *fala*. Not anymore. Our enchanters make do with the relics left after the Great War."

Danil nodded. "It was a silly hope."

"Hardly that." He looked at the parchment closely, casually tracing the scribblings. "Your task as custodian is to protect your leylines. They chose you for a reason."

"Elania mentioned once that custodians are trained by their predecessor."

Hafryn raised an eyebrow. "Not exactly helpful for us, is it?"

Danil folded his arms. A lump of unease formed in his throat. "Hafryn, I don't know what I'm doing."

Hafryn clasped his hand while indicating toward the surrounding forest. "You need only lift your eyes to see otherwise, *fala*. Or look down at the first crystal on your chest."

The crystal was a contented blue with striations of silver. It brightened to turquoise as if knowing it had Danil's attention.

Hafryn snorted. "See? You're the custodian of the deadlands. The leylines trust you to protect them." He tightened his grip. "Perhaps it's time you start trusting yourself as well."

Danil mustered a smile. "I'll try."

"That's a start, at least."

Danil hesitated, then motioned for Hafryn to hand back the parchment. "Here, join me."

The wolf followed him to the pebbled edge of the stream, where Danil set the parchment to the current. It spun lazily across the water's surface before being sucked down into the mine shaft. Hafryn watched it disappear, his expression bemused.

"Just in case," Danil said with a shrug.

EARLY MORNING LIGHT cast a soft shade of pink upon the canvas as Danil stared up at the tent ceiling. Hafryn lay curled beside him, his face wedged between the pillows and Danil's shoulder. He snored softly, his red hair free of its usual braid.

Soft footfalls indicated the arrival of a servant to light the brazier in the living quarters of their tent.

Danil sighed. It was tempting to just lay there, basking in the warmth of the familiar body beside him. He idly traced the freckles dotting Hafryn's bare arm. The wolf snuffled and burrowed deeper into the mound of pillows. Danil resisted a snort.

Pressing a kiss to the wild mess of hair, he gently eased himself out from under the blankets and went to their trunk in search of fresh breeches and a homespun shirt. Hafryn didn't stir as he pulled on his boots, and so Danil quietly slipped out into the living quarters in search of tea.

He frowned to find the servant nowhere in sight. The brazier remained unlit, the space undisturbed. His cloak was thrown haphazardly over the sprawl of cushions, the remnants of a late meal still on the desk.

Movement caught his eye. Perched on the edge of the desk was a massive, grey-winged owl. Far too big to be anything but a shifter, it nonetheless was strangely translucent, like a ghost. Danil made a warding sign as it glared at him with predatory intensity.

Wings flaring, it launched to attack.

Danil jerked back just as a blade whistled through the air from the shadows.

A woman leaped from behind the desk, another blade in her clenched fist. She bore the red tabard of the Roldaerian

Magi Guard, but the ghostly owl Trueform followed as if somehow tethered to her.

"Amasian," Danil snarled.

The woman bared her teeth. "Custodian."

A heartbeat later, she was on him. Danil rolled, narrowly avoiding the blade as she stabbed at his neck. They fetched up against the legs of the desk. She slashed his chest, slicing open his tunic and barely missing flesh. The crystal awakened to a blinding white.

Danil yelled, gripping the crystal. He stabbed upwards into his attacker's shoulder. Skin sizzled where the crystal bit deep.

The woman screamed in shock.

A red wolf suddenly slammed into her, and the desk toppled over with a crash. The woman scrambled backward before Hafryn was on her, fangs bared as he leaped at her throat. With a sickening crunch, bones snapped, and the woman fell limp.

The air about the wolf shimmered as Hafryn transformed. "Danil, did she cut you?" Hafryn turned him about, green eyes frantic. "Danil!"

Danil shook his head mutely. The crystal cast angry light about the tent.

Hafryn almost sagged in relief. "Elania must have missed her last night. Cursed Roldaerians."

"I saw her Trueform," Danil said numbly, staring at the dead woman.

Hafryn froze, his face paling in shock.

"Hafryn, she's Amasian."

~

"FOUR OF OUR SENTRIES ARE DEAD," Sonnen growled as he

entered the tent. "As are the guards outside. You have much to do to convince me this is not the work of Roldaer."

Danil and Hafryn shared a look.

The dead assassin had been moved onto the uprighted desk, where Elania and Blutark busily removed an accoutrement of blades and needle-like implements from her clothing. Magelights bobbed about the tent to glint off the weapons.

"She appears Roldaerian," Elania said as they reached the desk. She inspected the assassin's tunic. "This fabric is from the royal city, no less."

"Her dagger's also poisoned," Blutark noted, turning the blade toward the light. A black film thickly coated the edge. "A favored method of Roldaerian slayers." He tossed the blade into the brazier, where the flames hissed and crackled.

The rumble in Sonnen's chest deepened as he made to leave. "Let us see how Emissary Arlyn explains this."

"Sonnen, wait," Hafryn said, stepping in front of him. "Arlyn can't know what's happened."

Danil quickly nodded. "If the emissary discovers I was attacked, she could use it against us. I don't believe that this woman is Roldaerian."

The dragon prince frowned in confusion before his gaze dropped to the angrily glowing crystal against Danil's tunic. "Your crystal has tasted blood, custodian."

He wondered if it was as bad an omen as he suspected. "Amasian blood, no less."

Together with Hafryn, he quickly recounted the events of the attack, careful to describe the Trueform he'd seen.

Sonnen grimaced and shook his head in denial. "That cannot be. Hafryn, did you also see this owl?"

Hafryn shook his head. "I woke to find Danil fighting for his life."

With a cold rush, Danil realized seeing the ghostlike owl had likely saved his life. "It's like I could see both her and her Trueform at the same time," he said. "That's how I avoided the first blade."

Sonnen rubbed his chin. "The ability to see both shifter and Trueform is not a gift I'm familiar with. Can you see our Trueforms now?"

Glancing about the tent, Danil shook his head. "I don't know how I did it," he admitted ruefully.

"Perhaps the ability revealed itself because there was a need," Blutark mused as he tapped a blade restlessly against his thigh.

"Or it's somehow connected to the first crystal," Elania said. "It did come to your aid when she attacked you, Danil."

The crystal's agitated glow softened a little under the praise.

"Well, there's one way to confirm if this assassin is Amasian," Hafryn muttered, moving to the desk. The wolf shifter bent close over the body, examining between the woman's fingers and then her armpits. Muttering under his breath, he turned to her scalp.

"What are you looking for?" Danil asked as he peered over Hafryn's shoulder.

"All Houses have a glyph," Sonnen said, arms folded as he watched. "If she's an owl as you say, she'll belong to House of Eyrie."

The House glyph on Danil's own palm shined as if freshly painted. "What does a House glyph have to do with whether she's an owl or not?"

"The Eyrie is the only House to which owls are born," Elania uttered, face grim in the magelight. "They're the assassins of Amas, and they pride themselves in never letting a contract go unfulfilled."

"Contract?" Danil blanched in alarm.

"Let's not get ahead of ourselves," Blutark muttered with a placating gesture. "Even if she is Eyrie, we can't know for certain that Danil was her target."

Danil said dully, "She called me custodian."

Flames showed in Sonnen's eyes.

Hafryn straightened, his mouth thin. "Well, there it is." He pointed.

Behind the woman's left ear was a tiny glyph no larger than a fingernail. Surprisingly delicate, it comprised of concentric waves and small florets in a tight, repeating pattern.

"I know this glyph," Danil murmured, trying to recall where he had seen it.

"Of course you do, *fala*," Hafryn said. With a sigh, he pulled back the sleeve of his tunic to reveal the inside of his elbow. A matching symbol lay there, small and gleaming pale blue.

Danil gaped in astonishment.

Hafryn lowered his sleeve. "I'm of the House of Eyrie."

4

"You said you're from the High Reaches," Danil blurted out. "Why didn't you tell me?"

Hafryn spread his hands apologetically. "The High Reaches are within Eyrie territory. I don't associate with my kin anymore, *fala*. I wasn't exactly suited to the role of assassin."

"You still bear their glyph," Danil objected. He knew how glyphs worked—they stayed until their magic was spent. For House glyphs, it was when the bearer rescinded their connection or became part of a new House. Or died.

Hafryn grimaced. "One doesn't generally leave the Eyrie. I've stretched my luck already with my association with Corros."

The realization of how little Danil knew of the man burned deep. "Did she attack me because I'm with you?" he asked with an effort.

"Unlikely, *fala*. The Eyrie aren't generally motivated by emotion."

Sonnen grunted in agreement. "The House of Eyrie is renowned for fixing problems for a fee, Danil. Owls are unique due to their hunting abilities, keen eyesight, and silent wings. They are formidable assassins and rarely fail."

"Someone *paid* for the Eyrie to kill me?" Danil asked, dumbfounded. He sat heavily on a chest, his stomach unsettled.

"A contract would have been made with a Keeper," Hafryn muttered. He scrubbed his hair. "Keepers handle all assignations and decide who to send out. No one acts as sole agents—at least, not for long."

"But why come after me at all?" Danil asked, feeling a chill in his bones. He'd never given it much thought, but there had to be Amasians who hated humans as surely as the Roldaerian magi hated shifters.

"The border lies a great distance away for many Amasians," Sonnen replied, expression perturbed. "There are some on the High Council who argue that protecting the deadlands is not an Amasian fight." He raised his hand when Danil opened his mouth to protest. "I speak for everyone here when I say that is not our thinking, Danil."

Danil folded his arms, thinking hard. "That's why you're back so soon. You think the High Council will decide against sending aid."

"We have allies—perhaps enough to make a difference," Sonnen replied. He studied the dead woman and released a disconsolate sigh. "You were right to seek discretion. Should the Roldaerians discover Amas is not united, the magi will quickly grow bold."

Danil thought of what Magus Brianna had almost wrought in her bid to possess mage-crystals. He chafed his arms against the chill.

Hafryn scrubbed his face in agitation. "But the assassin had known what Danil is. Murdering custodians is anathema to all Amasians, including the Eyrie."

"Maybe it's because I'm human," Danil whispered dully.

Hafryn scowled. "What? No—"

"He makes a fair point, Hafryn," Blutark countered. "Not all Amasians are so enamored by humans."

Elania made a soft sound of contemplation. "Even fewer believe a human could be custodian, least of all to a land that has been dead of all magic and life for centuries—no disrespect meant, Danil."

"None taken," he replied dourly.

Hafryn gaped at them.

"It is why I returned here, rather than continue to privately broker for the support of our councilors," Sonnen muttered. His gaze returned to Danil. "You must stand before the High Council in Corros and be heard. You are the best suited to helping them understand what is happening here."

Danil shook his head in denial. Only months ago he had been little more than a deadland scavenger under the thumb of the magi. "I'm no diplomat, Sonnen," he argued. "I'll make things worse."

Sonnen gave a mild smile. "Let them see who you are, custodian. It will be enough."

Danil snorted in disbelief.

"What of the assassin?" Hafryn argued. "Once Danil's enemies realize they've failed, they'll send others. He won't be safe in Corros."

"Nor is he safe here, but in Corros we have a greater chance of protecting him while also identifying who ordered his death. However, we must act as if the attack this morning never occurred," Sonnen said.

Elania's eyes narrowed. "You've decided to take the emissary to the High Council as well," she guessed. "The

Roldaerians can't know that there are Amasians who oppose our presence in the deadlands."

Sonnen inclined his head. "I'm to breakfast with Emissary Arlyn now and let her know the High Council has agreed to a meeting. Danil and Hafryn, you will join me." He paused to study Danil. "You had best change out of that tunic, custodian."

Danil abruptly noticed the rents in the fabric. Mustering a nod, he headed for the partition separating the sleeping quarters from the rest of the tent. He pulled out a new tunic, pausing only to wipe the crystal clean of any remnant blood. Taking a slow, calming breath, Danil released it and watched the stone settle into pale blue.

He returned to find Hafryn checking his blade before sliding it into a sheath on his belt. For the first time, the wolf appeared rattled.

"*Fala*," he began.

"Not now," Danil murmured, forcing down the hurt at Hafryn keeping secrets.

They joined Sonnen in his trek across camp to an orange tent edged with glyphs marking the House of Corros. Inside, the Roldaerian emissary was already seated at a small table laden with plates of meat, bread, and fruits.

Arlyn rose and curtseyed. "Good morning to you all."

"Emissary Arlyn," Sonnen said. "I trust you slept well."

She smiled. "I confess to being unused to such rudimentary accommodations, but my comfort was seen to most kindly."

"I'm pleased," Sonnen said, then motioned for her to sit.

With just four chairs at the table, Danil found himself seated beside the emissary. Hafryn sat opposite him, eyebrow raised.

"This is quite the feast, Your Highness," Arlyn said

happily as she filled her plate with food. "Far grander than I was told to expect given the circumstances."

Sonnen speared a slice of ham onto his plate. "What circumstances do you refer to, emissary?"

She set down her fork. "Please, we can be informal—call me Arlyn."

The dragon prince inclined his head, but Danil noted he didn't offer Arlyn the same informality.

Arlyn smiled again. "I speak of the deadlands, Your Highness. Many of my people have succumbed to the dangerous pits and tunnels that stretch all the way to Amas. These strange new gullies aside, much of the land is a bleak and desolate place unfit for habitation." She placed a hand on Danil's arm. "I'm sure you agree, dear Danil."

Danil resisted the urge to pull his arm loose. "Not so much, emissary." He noticed Hafryn eyeing him with amusement. "There are some with the skill to safely traverse the deadlands, although most people know better than to try."

"Hmm, quite so," Arlyn murmured. "I imagine your experience is unique, given where you were born." She turned back to Sonnen. "But I must ask, Your Highness. Are we safe here? I heard quite the commotion earlier."

Danil's grip on his fork slipped. Across from him, Hafryn threw him a quelling look.

Sonnen's expression remained carefully blank as he peeled an orange into segments. "We are surrounded by scree fields, Emissary Arlyn. Perhaps you heard one giving way."

"I see." She returned to her plate.

"It's a dangerous place, as you say, Arlyn," Hafryn muttered. He stabbed a slice of meat with more force than necessary. "Perhaps you should relay that back to your armies. We know they're gathering at the royal city."

"Hafryn," Sonnen chided.

Hafryn's eyes widened innocently. "Oh, we're not done mincing words yet? My apologies." His smile showed teeth.

Arlyn's eyes gleamed with amusement. "No, he speaks fairly, Your Highness. It's true King Liam is a man open to many contingencies. It's my hope we can avoid the unpleasantness of war."

Hafryn muttered something under his breath.

Sonnen ignored his friend. "Amas would similarly prefer a diplomatic solution. The High Council has sent word that they will hear your terms. Transport will be ready later this morning."

"Wonderful." Arlyn beamed. "May I have my attendants? The two I brought with me shall suffice." Her face was both open and firm, set to bargain.

Sonnen merely nodded. "I will have word sent to your remaining attendants, emissary."

Arlyn once again squeezed Danil's arm. "How very wonderful. I do hope you'll excuse my enthusiasm, Danil, but I never expected to enter Amas. This will be quite the adventure!"

DANIL SHOVED his tunics into a pack.

The tent was quiet save for the soft 'snick' of Hafryn checking over each of his blades before the wolf stashed them in various locations on his body. The desk was clear once again, the assassin's body taken away to be hidden from curious eyes.

One of Elania's protective glyphs made lazy circles

around the central tent pole. The crystal hanging from Danil's neck took on the same golden light, singing low in the back of his mind.

Behind him, Hafryn sighed. "The emissary is a friendly sort, no?"

With an effort, Danil turned to see the wolf shifter perched on the trunk at the end of the pallet. Hafryn clasped his hands between his knees, his head bowed.

"Arlyn wants me to be her ally."

"A smart move for when we get to Corros," Hafryn muttered.

Setting aside his pack, Danil said, "Maybe. If she truly wants what we do."

"You don't think so?"

Danil sat beside Hafryn on the pallet. "It's like you said —King Liam might have sent Arlyn here, but he's is still preparing for war. Arlyn will use the threat of Roldaer's armies to demand concessions from the High Council." He gave a deep sigh. "I doubt we'll like her demands."

"I can remain here if you wish. Keep an eye on the border."

Startled, Danil turned to fully face Hafryn. The wolf's mouth was downturned but determined, and Danil swore he saw lines of tension about his eyes. "I don't want to go to Corros without you," he replied after a moment.

Green eyes searched Danil's face. "I should have told you, though. About Eyrie."

Swallowing carefully, he managed, "It came as a surprise."

"And an unpleasant one at that." Hafryn looked irritated with himself. "You might have guessed the Eyrie are a secretive lot. We don't reveal our Trueforms, not even to those we hold beloved. Shifting is learned in private so that our owls remain hidden and able to perform their tasks."

"That must make the other Houses suspicious of you," Danil murmured.

Hafryn shrugged. "It's something you grow accustomed to." He clasped his hands together. "I'd shown certain characteristics of owls as a child—I could sneak up on folk, catch them unawares. I never brawled with other younglings, instead preferring to bide my time. Folk began to talk."

"They expected you to be an owl."

Hafryn nodded. "Transforming into a wolf when I was ten summers old came as an unpleasant shock. I was so certain the gods had made a mistake that I transformed before the main hall in my village and demanded I be trained regardless." He shrugged. "I was exiled instead."

Danil was appalled at their harshness. "You were a child, Hafryn."

"I'd revealed my Trueform and therefore was of no use to my House. I was damned lucky to be given exile." His mouth ticked upwards in an echo of a smile. "So I wandered for a time, worked when I could and stole more often than needed. Sonnen found me working in a caravan and offered me a meal. When he left the next day, I followed."

Danil wondered if he'd ever be that resourceful or determined. He reached across and took Hafryn's hand, squeezing it gently.

"Forgive me for not telling you sooner," Hafryn murmured. "I bear the Eyrie glyph not out of pride, *fala*. It's so that I never forget the people who decided my Trueform wasn't enough."

It was something Danil could understand.

5

A short while later a blue dragon circled down off the mountain peak, large wings outstretched as it glided over the deadlands. It landed on the stretch of rock in a flurry of dust and dislodged pebbles, a small carrier box in its talons. Danil shielded his eyes against the grit.

His vision cleared to see a plain-faced young man stand where the dragon had been. Danil recognized him from Altonas as Sonnen's distant cousin, Griff.

Sonnen strode across to greet the young man, and for a moment Danil saw a ghostly blue dragon, steam drifting up from its nostrils as a golden dragon flared its wings.

Then the sight was gone. Danil paused.

"Is something wrong, Danil?" Arlyn asked brightly, coming to stand beside him. She looked resplendent in a fur-lined cloak and red robe with heavy brocade at her neck. Her pale hair was pulled up and dotted with matching ruby gems.

"Dust got in my eye, emissary," Danil murmured.

The two Roldaerian attendants waited beside an

oversized chest, their faces carefully blank. While still armored, their cloaks were new and delicately embroidered.

Arlyn followed his gaze. "Ah. Prince Sonnen was kind enough to have my trunk brought to me." She winked at him. "Can't stand before the High Council looking like a scavenger nation, can we?"

Her reference to Danil's past annoyed him, and he resisted a scowl. "I suppose not."

She beamed at him.

Hafryn sauntered up the gravel path with Elania and Blutark, deep in conversation. Neither enchanter carried travel packs with them.

"Excuse me, emissary," Danil said as he stepped away. He hurried to join his friends as they reached the pennants marking the top of the camp. "You're not coming?" he asked Elania and Blutark.

Elania shook her head. "There is not much we can personally do to sway the Council to aid in the protection of the deadlands. We can, however, watch over it in your absence. While other enchanters are up to that task, we figured you'd prefer folk you know."

A knot in his belly eased. "Thank you," he swallowed hard.

The bear shifter winked. "Just ask the leylines to hold off on making more crystals, eh? At least until you're back."

"I'll try," Danil said with a crooked smile. "They're pretty willful, though."

Hafryn bumped his shoulder. "Like their custodian."

"We'll send updates, but you'll likely already know if anything is amiss," Blutark said, nodding to the crystal dangling off Danil's neck. The stone flashed a cheerful green in response.

Elania pressed a kiss to Danil's cheek. "Don't be so

worried, Danil. You'll discover friends in Corros, I'm sure of it."

"Hopefully they're on the High Council," Hafryn quipped.

Feeling a jostle of nerves in his belly, Danil glanced over at Griff. The blue dragon shifter seemed intent on ignoring them. "Didn't Griff have a bigger carrier box last time he transported people?"

Hafryn grinned. "That's for our army contingents. Don't worry, though. Griff has strong talons."

Danil hadn't given much thought to how they'd reach Corros, but he was confident that he didn't want the dour blue dragon to take him. His gaze slid to Sonnen as the two dragons approached. He wondered if Sonnen could take them instead.

"Dragons don't like to be used as chattel, Danil. Royals even less so," Hafryn remarked, mouth quirking as he read Danil's expression. "It offends their sensibilities."

"Indeed, Hafryn." Sonnen bared his teeth in a humorless grin. "My cousin knows his duties," he added, golden eyes moving to Griff. "I will see you all safely at the waypoint tonight."

The young man bowed. "Yes, my prince."

With that, Sonnen transformed into a golden dragon so huge it blotted out Danil's vision of the sky. Massive wings unfurled, and then Sonnen launched into the air in a swirl of angry dust.

"You insulted him," Danil mused as the dragon quickly became a golden speck amidst the clouds.

Hafryn huffed a laugh. "His scales are thick, *fala*." He slung his pack over one shoulder and turned to Griff. "Shall we?"

The air about the young man shimmered as the blue

dragon took form. This close, Danil could see the glittering white of the dragon's underbelly. Griff waited beside the carrier, staring down his long snout at them. Made primarily of wood, the carrier was a square box held together by metal straps that gleamed with enchanted glyphs. Danil quietly hoped the enchantments had been recently renewed.

Arlyn eyed the dragon and carrier dubiously.

Hafryn smiled at her discomfort and bowed. "You first, emissary." His eyeteeth seemed inexplicably longer.

She sniffed before climbing the short ramp, her attendants in tow.

"Best of luck, Danil," Blutark murmured, sparing the younger man a quick hug that took him by surprise. "You'll do well in Corros."

Taking a steadying breath, Danil nodded. They all knew what was at stake. He joined Hafryn on the ramp. Inside, a dozen rope handholds were bolted to the walls, and to Danil's relief, shuttered portholes dotted the walls.

The ramp rose up and closed behind them, flooding the carrier in darkness. Momentarily blinded, Danil's vision shifted. A ghostly red wolf stood beside him. Its edges appeared limned with light. Danil reached out, curious, and suddenly found Hafryn's sleeve.

"Steady your feet," Hafryn murmured, guiding Danil's hand toward one of the rope holds.

The harsh grate of claws on wood echoed in the dark around them, and then the ground bucked. Danil gripped tight, stomach plummeting as the carrier yawed sideways and then rocketed up into the sky.

Hafryn cursed beside him, but after a few terrifying heartbeats, the carrier steadied. The air vibrated with the roar of a dragon.

"Griff's normally more graceful than that," Hafryn muttered. He banged his fist against the wall in protest at the blue dragon, and then slid a shutter open to blue sky and a buffeting wind. The sudden brightness made the freckles across Hafryn's nose and cheeks more apparent.

Hafryn opened the shutter beside Arlyn also, who still had the ropehold in a white-knuckled grip. She murmured her thanks.

Danil peered out. The deadlands quickly grew tiny below them, the black rocks broken up by seams of verdant green within the canyons and ravines. They circled over the camp, the tents becoming bright spots of reds, blues, and yellows. A humming energy drew Danil's gaze toward a location between Roldaer and Amas, where deep underground lay the temple that the halfbreed Kaul had made for himself. He sensed the leylines coursing underneath, filled with power.

The mountains swung into view, all sharp peaks and jagged edges. With a whomp of powerful wings, Griff sailed over the first jagged ridge, where snow still lay heavy despite it being early spring. More mountains stretched out ahead, their valleys dense with forest.

Hafryn returned to revel in the view, standing on the tip of his toes to peer down. The wind whipped his braid back and forth.

"That way lies Altonas, *fala*." Hafryn pointed southward, where more dense forest carpeted the ground far below. "A half day's flight by dragon-wing."

Danil followed his gaze. It had taken them days traveling on foot to reach the broken citadel of Altonas in their quest to uncover Magus Brianna's plans. In that time, Hafryn had revealed himself as more than a trickster wolf with a penchant for thievery.

"And ahead lies Corros," Hafryn added, releasing a sigh as he took in the mountains and low-scudding clouds on the horizon.

Danil studied Hafryn instead. The green of his eyes appeared muted. "Do you really like Corros so little?" he asked quietly.

The wolf leaned against the wall, arms folded. Arlyn and her two attendants seemed absorbed by the view from the opposite porthole.

"Corros is my home, but my association with Sonnen draws me closer to the citadel's politicking than I like." Hafryn shrugged. "It led me to seek a few rotations on the deadlands—not a terrible outcome, I must admit." An edge of a smile tugged his mouth as his eyes roamed Danil's face.

"Being with a human won't cause you trouble?" Danil asked.

"Our issue is with Roldaer, not with humans." Hafryn hesitated before conceding, "There are folk who don't know the difference, but you won't find them in Corros. Sonnen doesn't abide such narrow-minded folk." He looked over the landscape, frowning in thought. "Human or no, custodians are honored in Corros, and you won't be ignored. We'll soon discover who's on our side, and those who may be swayed."

"How many of the High Council do we need on our side?"

"It's a majority vote of those present. There are twelve council members, one from each House. We're fortunate that Corros is hosting the meeting, or this could be a very long trip."

"Maybe we can get the High Council to inspect the deadlands, see how it's changed," Danil suggested.

"I expect some will be quite open to the idea," Hafryn said. "The Eliar and Jolun Houses border the Orineye Sea—

much of their trade is with human folk. They understand better than most the threat of the magi. Most other Houses are inland and have little interaction or care for what happens beyond Amas." He leaned against the porthole, squinting against the buffeting wind. "Amas won't sit idle should Roldaer invade. But we must convince them to make their stand in the deadlands."

Danil nodded. If the Roldaerian magi gained control of the deadlands, they could use the leylines just like Magus Brianna planned.

"Decisions of the High Council aren't always driven by what is good or obvious," Hafryn muttered, eyes flicking to Arlyn. "At least the Eyrie councilor won't be there. He rarely concerns himself with the larger issues of Amas."

"But there will still be Eyrie in Corros," Danil guessed.

"Aye, as personal guards to other the High Council members and those who can afford their fee." Hafryn crinkled his nose. "I have little doubt they report all goings-on to the Eyrie councilor anyway."

"Maybe I'll be able to discover who among them have owl Trueforms," Danil murmured, determined to learn how to use his strange new gift at will.

"Good plan, *fala*. Just remember to conceal your abilities —owls aren't the only dangerous shifters in Amas."

Danil already knew that. He'd seen his friends fight.

The sun sat low when they finally wheeled down a sheer cliff face and into a valley. Sonnen landed in a clearing, his golden scales a flash of light in the fading day before the dragon transformed. Griff set the carrier down carefully and Danil gladly stepped out onto the grass to join Sonnen by a ring of charred stones that marked a campfire. Just beyond was a stone marker with whorled glyphs etched into the rock. The glyphs grew brighter as he approached.

"This is a common waypoint for folk crossing the mountains," Sonnen said in greeting. "It is said that Aramanth, the first dragon of Corros, rested in this clearing on her journey to discover the citadel."

"Fascinating." Arlyn inspected the marker. At her touch, the glyphs winked out.

Sonnen rumbled. "The wayfarer stone recognizes allies of Corros, emissary. When we reach the citadel, you would do well not to touch the glyphs or kiandrite, lest your message of peace be lost."

She flushed slightly. "Of course, Your Highness. I meant no insult."

Turning his back, Sonnen said, "Griff, you have first watch."

The blue dragon launched back into the air. He wheeled over the camp once before gliding in a broader, lazy circle.

"First watch for what?" Danil asked as he scanned their surroundings. The chance of attack from Roldaer was doubtful here.

Hafryn dumped his pack by the stones. "Mountain lions and the like."

"*Real* mountain lions?" Arlyn took a step back toward the carrier.

"Of course." Mirth showed in Hafryn's green eyes. "Not every creature in Amas is a shifter. Quite the opposite, in fact."

"I never gave it much thought," Danil murmured, glancing at the nearby pine trees. "Does that mean shifters run with animals?"

"Some Houses allow it, though in others it's frowned upon." Hafryn grinned. "I ran with a pack of timber wolves for a whole summer before Sonnen suggested if I was that bored I could do a stint on the deadlands."

Arlyn tilted her head. "You didn't forget who you were? After all that time?"

"We don't lose ourselves to the shift, emissary," he chided and was rewarded by another embarrassed flush. "Our Trueforms are just another aspect of ourselves." Hafryn tilted his head in thought. "Though I must admit I still get a hankering for raw game on occasion—grouse in particular, even if the feathers always got stuck between my teeth."

Danil resisted the urge to shudder.

Arlyn frowned. "Forgive my ignorance, but how do you know you aren't eating another Amasian?"

Hafryn huffed in bemusement. "We have our ways. Contrary to Roldaerian fables, I promise no one has accidentally served up a friend for dinner."

The emissary looked mildly disbelieving.

Turning to Danil, Hafryn said, "Let's get some firewood. I can smell ice on the wind."

"I'll join you," Sonnen said.

Hafryn raised an eyebrow but nodded.

They walked the granite outcrop into the trees. Back at the camp, Arlyn laid out her cloak on the ground before sitting, her two attendants silently watching the woods.

Danil's gaze slid to the horizon, where Griff was a black silhouette against the setting sun.

Sonnen also watched the blue dragon. "If the thermals are kind, we will be at Corros tomorrow." He broke apart a fallen branch for kindling.

"Not much time to prepare Danil for the High Council," Hafryn muttered.

Sonnen grunted. "Our Roldaerian emissary should prove a distraction. I expect any treaty she presents won't be accepted by the High Council."

"She'll demand kiandrite," Danil said, remembering her fixation on the crystal about his neck.

"That will only make the magi more powerful. The High Council will never agree to it," Sonnen said with a firm shake of his head.

"Hafryn thinks I should hide my ability to see Trueforms," Danil remarked.

Sonnen studied Danil, golden eyes knowing. "Then it has happened more than once."

"This morning."

Hafryn gave a grunt of surprise as Danil described what he'd seen during their departure.

Sonnen looked contemplative. "Until we know the extent of this new gift, it would be best you kept it hidden."

"You think there's more to it?" Danil asked as he tucked a large stick under his arm for the fire.

"Perhaps," Sonnen said. "Your new ability coincides with the emergence of the first crystal—I don't hold that to mere happenstance."

"The crystal could be responsible," Danil guessed.

"Or proximity to the deadlands," Sonnen countered. "But there is also your own abilities, Danil. You survived a magi curse because there is an innate power within you. You may find yourself called upon to use it."

"That's suitably alarming," Hafryn said with a frown. "What trouble are you flying us into, Sonnen?"

"The assassin is an added complication," Sonnen admitted. His golden eyes gleamed as he met Hafryn's gaze. "I expect you to hunt down the contract and the person who issued it."

"Of course," Hafryn dismissed his request as a foregone conclusion.

"The assassin may have targeted Danil, but I suspect the attack has more to do with the deadlands. Many have debated over who holds rights over it."

"No one does," Danil said. As the strip of land separating the borders of Roldaer and Amas, the deadlands had been in limbo for centuries.

"And everyone," Sonnen countered. His golden eyes seemed to brighten. "The leylines running beneath the deadlands are of Amasian origin. That is what the High Council needs to remember—as does all of Amas."

"I don't know if anything I say will be enough," Danil stated, feeling a slow wash of fear.

"You have served my House faithfully, even at great

personal cost, Danil." The dragon raised his palm, showing the whorled House glyph on his palm. It glittered gold as if lit from within. "No matter the outcome with the High Council, my House will not abandon you."

The glyph on Danil's own palm burned in acknowledgment.

7

They set off early the next morning, with frost still coating the outside of the carrier box. Hafryn seemed to revel in the flight, hands gripping the porthole as Griff glided over mountain peaks heavy with snow. Sonnen occasionally drifted into view, his powerful wings stretched wide as he rode the thermals.

Dusk saw them descend over a series of grey spires on the edge of a sprawling lake that was a startling blue against the jagged rocks and ice. Only when they drew near did Danil realize the spires were unnatural.

Each spire was an intricate series of large and smaller towers, some with painted roofs or bearing pennants of gold. From their vantage, Danil could see stone courtyards, arched gateways and balconies large enough for a fully shifted dragon. Battlements and small bolt holes made him wonder what sort of enemies Corros had once fought, but then his eyes caught on a flock of birds that shot from a tower to spiral down to the lake below. A harbour town sat on the edge of the lake. A handful of wooden piers and pontoons jutted out into the water, where boats and skiffs sat anchored.

Griff wheeled them between two spires connected by a bridge suspended high above the earth. They landed on a sprawling platform with a whorled design inset into the marble.

The carrier opened, and Danil stepped out gratefully and turned in a slow circle. An arched entry led into the keep of the largest tower, its buttresses engraved with winged folk and unfamiliar symbols. Head tilting upwards, Danil counted dozens of balconies and huge windows filtering sunlight into the tower's interior.

Arlyn stepped down beside him, her expression resolute. The crest of Roldaer gleamed on her chest.

Whoops of laughter came from an adjacent platform, and Danil watched in astonishment as a group of younglings flung themselves from the edge only to transform mid-fall into exotically colored birds. Their raucous shrieks echoed amongst the towers.

"Parrots," Hafryn muttered in fond exasperation. "Welcome to Corros, the great citadel of the east," he added, stretching his arms expansively. "More than sixty generations of Amasians have lived here, ever since the great dragon Aramanth first roosted here in a winter cave."

Danil peered past the ornate pillars lining the entrance to the keep. He imagined a massive and immutable creature within, golden eyes glowing like magelights.

Still in his dragon form, Griff lifted off from the platform and winged down to disappear into a lower keep.

"Have dragons always ruled here?" Arlyn asked, glancing about. Her eyes momentarily lingered on a vein of kiandrite threading innocuously across the platform.

"In one manner or another," Hafryn said. "Sonnen comes from a long and honored lineage."

A party of Amasians made their way out of the keep. At their lead was a woman in officious blue robes, flanked by House guards bearing the Corros glyph on their breast. They carried spears displaying the gold pennant of Sonnen's House.

The officious woman reached them and bowed. "Lady Arlyn of Roldaer, I am Naril, clerk to Councilor Tresa of Corros. I trust your journey was acceptable."

Arlyn inclined her head and smiled warmly. "A unique way to travel to be sure, but satisfactory."

"Excellent. Councilor Tresa apologizes for not greeting you herself, but we have rooms prepared for you, my lady." Naril bowed again. "If you'll come this way."

Startled at being summarily ignored, Danil stepped back as the House guards moved to escort Arlyn. A flash of gold showed on the horizon.

"Ah, here comes our dragon prince," Hafryn said, his voice carrying across the platform. "It would be remiss of you not to welcome Prince Sonnen home, wouldn't you say, Naril?"

The officious clerk slowed. Her expression turned cautious. "As you say."

Buzzing with nervous energy, Danil watched the golden speck grow large and distinct with massive wings that cut powerfully through the air. Sonnen eventually landed beside them, scarcely alighting before transforming into his human form. His tunic was once again heavily embroidered, his breeches dark with seams of gold. His eyes showed flames as he took in the clerk and escort.

Naril bowed deeply as Sonnen approached. "Welcome home, my prince."

The golden dragon scarcely acknowledged at her. "Where is Councilor Tresa?"

Naril gave a polite smile. "She's in meetings at the moment, my prince."

Sonnen scowled. "The High Council has adjourned until week's end," he argued.

"Yes, my prince, as you say. A few councilors have stayed on to discuss certain events," Naril said.

"How many?"

"Beg pardon?" Her smile slipped a little.

"How many councilors are attending the meeting?"

Naril almost squirmed. "I don't—I'm not privy to that information, Your Highness. I'm certain the meetings are nothing of high importance, however." She attempted a new smile.

"But important enough to ignore the arrival of the custodian of the deadlands," Sonnen observed. The flames in his eyes deepened.

The clerk swallowed thickly. "I'm certain no slight was intended, Your Highness. Time must have gotten the better of them."

"I see." Sonnen studied the small contingent of House guards set to escort Arlyn. "And are my House guards likewise preoccupied? You appear to be missing half your retinue, Naril."

The clerk's mouth opened.

Sonnen raised his hand. "You are either impertinent or incompetent, Naril. Either is intolerable when it means Custodian Danil is without attendants from my House. Am I likewise to find no rooms prepared for him?"

Naril's face turned bright red as she stammered. "W-we expected the custodian would prefer to share Hafryn of Eyrie's rooms."

Danil muttered under his breath, "Gods, yes."

Hafryn snorted.

The flames grew in Sonnen's eyes. "Have Councilor Tresa meet me in my quarters. Now."

"But—"

Sonnen's expression darkened

Naril bowed deeply. "Of course, my prince. Immediately."

With a low growl, the dragon prince swept past her, motioning for Danil and Hafryn to follow.

Danil felt the heat of Arlyn's gaze on the back of his neck as he trotted to catch up.

Entering the keep, the bracing cold of the mountains was suddenly tempered by warmth and the rustle of foliage. Sunlight streamed in through the grand archways, alighting on massive trees whose thick branches stretched up through gaps in the high ceiling. Magelights the size of Danil's thumbnail bobbed and weaved between the tree roots and leaves and twinkled prettily. A causeway and stairs led up to a simple throne looked over by an obsidian stone dragon.

Hafryn and Sonnen seemed unaffected by the grandeur of the place. With an effort, Danil stopped himself from gaping.

"What was that, Sonnen?" Hafryn growled under his breath as they entered a corridor where long veins of kiandrite cast iridescent light. "You told us the High Council had asked for Danil."

"There was a vote," Sonnen muttered. "Not all saw the need."

"Let me guess—our own councilor was one of them," Hafryn spat derisively.

Sonnen led them through a cavernous hall of polished stone. Amasians were visible on the upper causeways.

"Tresa raised doubts with me in private. However, I did not think she would slight Danil by ignoring his arrival entirely." His eyes showed flames. A few people sketched hurried bows while giving him a wide berth. "It is nothing that cannot be handled."

"I'd still prefer to stay with Hafryn," Danil declared. "If that's allowed, of course," he added hastily.

"It is. And the insult will be dealt with. Tonight. We shall have a feast to honor the arrival of the deadlands' first custodian."

Danil shot the dragon prince an alarmed look.

The flames in Sonnen's eyes eased a little. "Fear not, Danil. It will be among allies and friends. You will not have to test your wits against the High Council just yet."

It hardly settled his nerves, but Danil nodded gamely.

"Then I will see you tonight." Sonnen gave them a short bow before sweeping down a wide passageway.

With a sigh, Hafryn said, "This way, *fala*. We'll go the long route. It seems the more eyes are on you, the better."

They entered a new hall and took a walkway that followed the curve of an ancient tree that was wider than even the old inn of Farin. Danil peered up at the tree's craggy height, doing his best to ignore the whispers as a pair of shifters paused in a doorway to watch.

He hurried to catch up to Hafryn. "Why do you think Naril risked Sonnen's wrath like that?" he asked quietly.

Hafryn shrugged as they entered a corridor where magelights sat embedded in sconces. "It's easier for folk to ignore a problem when it's not in their face."

"And I'm a problem."

"Sonnen has the right of things. The High Council has been able to dally because the deadlands are of little interest to many of them. It will be harder for them to ignore the threat of Roldaer with you in their midst, setting tongues wagging."

Hafryn took him through a stone arch leading into a cavernous hall. Rows of market stalls filled the space, some with ornate canvas awnings and others exposed to the breeze sweeping in from the open balcony on the eastern edge of the hall. Most of the shifters busied themselves with packing up for the day, although some stalls with bright and strange fruits and greens remained busy with customers.

Hafryn took them on a wandering path through the stalls. A display of throwing daggers and small blades caught his eye, and he picked up one with a simple hilt offset by a blue glass bauble above the grip. "What do you think, *fala*? It matches your kiandrite."

The crystal in question had somehow wormed its way out from beneath Danil's tunic. It glowed deep blue against his chest. By habit, Danil ran his thumb over it, watching as a trail of contented purple followed in the wake of his touch.

Beady-eyed, the shopkeeper observed the crystal, then Danil.

"It's a handsome dagger," Danil allowed, not sure if Hafryn was genuinely set on purchasing the blade.

With a grin, Hafryn set about haggling. Danil watched with growing amusement as Hafryn both lauded the shopkeeper for her workmanship and harangued her for attempting to swindle a visiting custodian.

In the end, the shopkeeper settled for a handful of silver coins and the parting of a tooled leather sheath. She set about closing her shop, muttering to herself as Danil adjusted the blade to his belt.

Green eyes bright, Hafryn hooked an arm about Danil's waist and steered him down the row of stalls. He bent close to murmur, "I'll bet you a gold crown that our shopkeeper will be telling all who'll listen about how you affected your kiandrite just by touching it."

Danil raised an eyebrow. "And that's to our benefit?"

"Of course," Hafryn said. "Custodians are renowned for their connection to kiandrite. We're merely showing that you're no different."

Danil snorted. "For someone who takes no pleasure in politics, you're certainly good at it."

"Gossip is the lifeblood of politics here, and the townspeople are no different," Hafryn said.

They followed a line of engraved columns that threaded through a communal eating hall and past smaller meeting rooms. Plants and vines grew from alcoves and cracks in the floor.

Danil hadn't given it much thought, but he hadn't expected Corros to be so alive. He said as much to Hafryn.

"Not so different to the deadlands, is it?" Hafryn replied with a wink.

A group of five newcomers entered the far end of the corridor. Danil noticed them immediately. All had red hair, their eyes varying shades of green. Each wore jerkins dyed bright turquoise, a silver glyph over their hearts.

Hafryn resolutely ignored them.

One of them muttered something under his breath as they passed.

Danil glanced over his shoulder, and for a heartbeat, he saw a pair of tawny owls accompanied by three russet wolves. One wolf bared her teeth in a silent snarl.

"Hafryn—"

"Leave it. They're personal guards for the House of Refel," Hafryn muttered.

Danil gaped. "They hire Eyrie assassins?" he hissed.

"What? No, we spoke of this, *fala*," Hafryn said with a

frown. "Plenty of Eyrie are hired as personal guards for other Houses, and there's no telling who among them are owls."

But Danil knew what he saw. Owl assassins resided in Corros.

8

Hafryn took him to a set of three rooms at the end of a quiet corridor threaded with seams of kiandrite.

The roots of an old tree made the floor uneven, the worn tile cracked in places but smooth underfoot. Inside, a battered couch sat in front of a small hearth, and sunlight filtered in through curtains that led to a balcony overlooking the bridge and lake below. Turning about, Danil took in shelves filled with ornaments and scrolls, with a set of chests pushed up against the back wall. A curved door led to sleeping quarters with a pallet heavily layered with furs. Opposite was an alcove with a deep wading pool carved out of the rock. Heat seeped up through his boots, and Danil studied with interest the black pebbles in the floor inlaid in the shape of a warming glyph.

Hafryn dropped his pack and collapsed onto the couch with a sigh. The lines about his eyes eased.

With a rush of understanding, Danil said, "These have been your rooms for a long time."

Hafryn smiled slightly. "When Sonnen offers sanctuary, he means it wholeheartedly."

Danil traced the glyph on his palm. It seemed brighter since Sonnen's reaffirming of it.

"Many wear the House of Corros upon their skin, but few have had it personally placed there by our dragon prince," Hafryn observed, watching him. "It'll make folk nervous."

"Why?"

Hafryn shrugged. "You received a great honor unasked, without any posturing or grand gestures. There are folk who will wonder at the sort of human who can achieve such things. It'll certainly have meaning for the High Council."

Danil hoped so. He'd yet to shake the unease at being apparently snubbed by the council members. He shook his thoughts loose. "Those Eyrie in the hallway—are they your close kin?"

An echo of a smile showed on Hafryn's face. "We Eyrie have distinctive coloring. But no, I can't say I know them."

"They seemed to know you," Danil pointed out.

Hafryn leaned back, stretching his long legs. "It's easy for Eyrie to identify the exile of Corros," he said dryly. "They take offence on principle."

Danil's throat tightened at the unfairness of it. The Eyrie had no idea what Hafryn had done for them and the rest of Amas.

Hafryn looked bemused. "It worries me less than you expect, *fala*." His green eyes sharpened slightly. "But what you said in the corridor—about owls. Did you have another vision?"

He hesitated. "I don't think they're quite visions. It's almost like I can see both aspects of an Amasian at the same time."

"And you saw an owl Trueform?"

Danil nodded. "Two, actually. The rest were wolves."

Hafryn rubbed his chin thoughtfully. "We'll let Sonnen know, but it's even more important to keep this ability hidden. We can't know what the Eyrie will do if they suspect their Trueforms are no longer secret."

"You're not worried that there are owls here?"

"They'll bear watching, but if their task has nothing to do with us, then you can expect to be ignored. The Eyrie pride themselves on restraint."

Danil turned back to the shelves of ornaments. "You speak like you're not one of them," he murmured. He picked up a small figurine of a bear, its likeness reminding him of Blutark.

"I'm not renowned for my Eyrie discipline," Hafryn said with a smirk.

Danil snorted. He set the figurine down, his eye catching on a tarnished belt buckle half-buried under a sheaf of papers. Pulling it out, Danil recognized the ancient Roldaerian script and battered edge. "What's this doing here?"

Hafryn craned his neck. "Hmm?"

"This belt buckle," Danil said, scraping the rust with his fingernail. "It's a relic from the Great War. I found it in the deadlands last summer." He turned about, eyebrow crooked. "You stole it from me."

"What?" Hafryn clumsily scrambled off the couch. "No, why would I do that?"

"I remember it clearly," Danil said, holding the buckle aloft. "You took it as payment when I had no kiandrite for you to steal."

Chagrined, Hafryn said, "We weren't exactly allies then, *fala*, and you were so easy to rile." A slight flush of pink showed on his cheeks. "Still, I must have forgotten to throw it away."

Danil fought off a grin and examined the row of shelves with greater interest. "Am I going to find a horde of stolen goods here, Hafryn?"

"Not as much as you think," the wolf muttered. "But maybe an item or two," he admitted begrudgingly.

Danil spied a collection of ancient arrowheads in a jar and grinned. "Well, I mind less now, knowing that you kept them."

Hafryn's mouth twitched. "That eases my mind immensely. But if you're done nosing through my secrets, we've a dinner to prepare for. Pretty sure I have a Balrani silk robe lying hereabouts that would suit you well—so long as we remove the tassels."

Danil suppressed a groan and trailed after him.

9

After a perfunctory wash, they emerged from the bathing pool to find clothes laid out for them on the sleeping pallet. To Danil's relief, a soft jerkin of fawn and dark breeches looked tailored to fit, and he wondered who'd managed to get such details. Hafryn's outfit was similar, with a green doublet which he matched with emerald earrings from a small box on the table.

Danil smoothed down the soft material of his jerkin in an effort to ease the fluttering in his belly.

Hafryn studied him, eyes warm. After a moment, he cleared his throat. "Let's not keep the everyone waiting, eh?"

Danil nodded. They left Hafryn's quarters and made their way across the maze of walkways and corridors. The swell of voices led them to a dining hall framed by a large oak tree similar to the ones growing wild about the camp back on the deadlands.

A steward at the door, dressed in a silk doublet and puffed sleeves, made them pause before they were announced.

"Hafryn of Eyrie, and Custodian Danil of the deadland tracts."

Sketching a bow, the steward opened the door and urged them inside.

Finely dressed Amasians already sat at the long tables, and Danil wondered if they were underlings or scions of the various Houses. The vaulted ceiling was softened by clinging ivy and magelights.

Danil made for a pair of empty seats at one of the lower tables, but a servant stopped him and instead guided him and Hafryn toward the raised table overlooking the rest of the hall.

Behind the table, a statue of a sleeping dragon carved from a huge slab of kiandrite reigned over the dining hall. It glowed soft pinks and yellows in the mellow light but soon brightened with blues and greens as Danil slowed to a stop before it in awe. It pulsed brightly, a gentle rippling of colors flaring from the dragon's chest and radiating to its wings. Its eyelids seemed to open to reveal irises of pure white, and Danil felt a strong presence welcoming him.

Hafryn touched his elbow and steered him toward a chair.

"Did you see that?" Danil hissed as a servant came to fill his glass with honeywine.

"I think everyone saw how Aramanth's statue reacted to you," Hafryn said, bemused as people whispered and pointed from their seats.

Trying not to flush, Danil said, "No, the eyes."

Hafryn frowned at him and shook his head.

Danil glanced back at the statue to find the dragon sleeping once more.

More Amasians filtered into the hall to take up the remaining seats. Sonnen arrived escorting a dark-haired woman resplendent in dark blue robes, her hair piled up high above her neck and interwoven with gold thread. She sat beside Danil, with Sonnen on her opposite side at the center of the table.

"Danil," Sonnen said, leaning forward. "This is Councilor Tresa of Corros. She speaks for the citadel on the High Council."

Danil mustered a polite nod, which Tresa returned. Golden baubles hung from her earlobes, catching in the light.

"Welcome to Corros, custodian," Tresa said, her voice a refined murmur. "Forgive me for not formally greeting you upon your arrival."

Danil smiled awkwardly. "Your welcome now is appreciated, Councilor Tresa."

Hafryn nodded to a servant who poured more honeywine into his glass. "It appears that we arrived earlier than expected."

Her smile slipped a little. "I assure you, Hafryn of Eyrie, we were quite prepared."

"Interesting," he tilted his head. "You ran quite a risk in insulting Custodian Danil with your preparations."

The woman stilled, frowning. She opened her mouth to speak but was interrupted as the steward's voice boomed across the dining hall once again.

"Lady Arlyn Nera, Emissary to Roldaer."

Arlyn entered wearing a crimson gown. The murmuring in the hall fell silent as she walked to the high table, her hands clasped demurely in front of her.

Sonnen rose from his seat and bowed. "Welcome, emissary."

Arlyn curtseyed. "Thank you for your kind hospitality, Your Highness."

He motioned to a chair a few seats further down from him.

With a slow, calming breath, Danil realized Arlyn was far enough away to be out of earshot. He wondered at the seating arrangements.

A soft bell chimed to indicate the start of the meal. Servants filtered into the hall with trays laden with bowls. Danil murmured his thanks as the soup was set before him, the creamy broth layered with mushrooms and herbs.

"Are the accommodations with Hafryn to your liking, custodian?" Sonnen said as he picked up a spoon. He ladled out a spoonful and nodded, and the hall was filled with conversation and the clink of cutlery.

Danil met the dragon prince's gaze, noting the gleam in his eyes. "They are, my prince."

"Call me Sonnen, Danil, as always," he replied.

Councilor Tresa raised a thoughtful eyebrow.

The chair beside Hafryn was pulled back, and a newcomer sat down. Danil turned to be snared by bright green eyes and a head of dark red hair. Freckles dusted the man's nose and cheeks, the red in his hair greying at the temples. The man smirked, eyes crinkling, and for a heartbeat, Danil saw what Hafryn would look like in another twenty summers. Behind the man was a ghostlike specter of a red wolf, one almost twice the size as Hafryn's own Trueform. It stood at guard, nose to the air and seeming to miss nothing in the great hall.

Then the vision was gone. Danil released a slow, calming breath.

The man ignored Danil, his gaze instead settling on Hafryn. "Cousin."

Danil mouthed the word at Hafryn.

Hafryn's lip curled, though he hardly looked at the

newcomer. "Viren." His jaw rippled, his hand tightening to a fist around his bread knife. "How unexpected to see you here."

Viren picked up a napkin and smoothed it over his lap. "It shouldn't be, cousin. I am Eyrie's member of the High Council, after all." He smiled, green eyes mild.

The red wolf flickered into Danil's sight again, closer than before. Although the man ignored him completely, the ghostly wolf now all but breathed against Danil's elbow. Seated, they were almost of a height. Danil held its gaze, suspecting that to baulk would be a mistake.

Back off, he told it.

A flicker of a frown crossed Viren's face.

"I was under the impression you were otherwise engaged, Viren," Hafryn muttered between clenched teeth. He threw a dark look down the table at Sonnen, but the dragon prince was engaged in conversation with two other shifters.

"Momentous times demand that all of Amas comes together," Viren said.

"Very noble of you," Hafryn muttered, tearing apart a hunk of bread with startling hostility.

Viren smiled. "Merely duty, cousin."

Danil wondered if Amasian etiquette allowed brawling during a meal, then peered beyond Tresa to the dragon prince. Sonnen seemed determined to ignore the two sniping wolves.

Tresa delicately cleared her throat. "Custodian. I'm told there was recently an incident on the deadlands," she said before taking a delicate sip of her soup.

Danil froze, startled. How did she know of the assassination attempt? He noticed Hafryn giving Tresa a carefully blank look.

"The Roldaerians," Tresa prompted. "They came upon you unexpectedly, I am told."

"A Roldaerian emissary speaking peace was certainly a surprise," Hafryn interjected, tone careful.

She smiled. "Certainly. But, tell me, how did they reach the deadlands without the knowledge of its custodian?"

Danil stilled as the conversation around them grew quiet. At the center of the table, a low rumble issued.

"It was Emissary Arlyn's party, councilor," Hafryn said. "They remained on Roldaerian land."

Tresa raised an eyebrow. "As I understand it, custodians have a sense of what happens across all of their lands. The custodian of Corros knows of happenings from here to the border and beyond."

Danil set down his spoon, feeling eyes on him. "Perhaps so, but custodians can sense only through their leylines— and the leylines of Corros have been established for millennia," Danil said. "The deadlands haven't had that luxury."

"Or perhaps your leylines are not as considerable as we have been led to believe," Tresa countered.

Danil frowned. "Kaul stole kiandrite from Amas to create those leylines, my lady. After his death, they were left buried and forgotten by all of Amas for centuries."

She opened her mouth to respond, but Danil raised a hand.

"Those of us who protect the deadlands are few— scarcely more than two score, as I am sure you are aware," he said firmly, his voice carrying. "And yet we are tasked with protecting an expanse of land that stretches for days. The leylines have lain untouched for centuries—is it your wish for the magi of Roldaer to have them?"

"Of course not," Tresa said with a serene smile. "But new leylines don't produce kiandrite."

"The leylines may be young, but the magic within them is as ancient as those running beneath your feet," Danil countered. Behind him, the statue of Aramanth pulsed brightly. "Not even your enchanters can predict what they will do."

She frowned at him, her eyes lingering on the kiandrite upon his chest as it matched the darkened blues and reds flashing across the crystal dragon.

Pushing down his annoyance, Danil added, "Regardless of how insignificant you may think the leylines of the deadlands are, they were once part of Amas. I'm here to ensure they are not abandoned by Amas a second time."

Tresa gave him an assessing look, and Danil felt the eyes of others from the tables below. He forced himself to hold the councilor's gaze.

Sonnen gave a contented rumble as servants came to clear the bowls for the next course. "The well of kiandrite chose Danil, and he has not flinched." His voice carried across the hall. "Nor can Amas, now that the leylines are free once more. It is up to the High Council to see the way forward."

Tresa nodded, mouth set. "Of course, my prince. We will do what is best for Amas. As always."

Beside Hafryn, Viren dabbed his mouth with a napkin. His green eyes gleamed as he studied the side of his kinsman's face. "I was surprised to hear of your involvement in the deadlands, cousin. You're quite diligent in serving the interests of Corros."

"It's a matter for all of Amas," Hafryn muttered. He turned his wine glass about in his hands. "Though I'm surprised to see you in Corros, *cousin*. Eyrie is a long way from here, and Roldaer's magi would have little interest in it should they invade."

"As you say," Viren said, eyes briefly flicking to Arlyn seated far down the table. "But war affects us all. I would prefer to know all avenues before committing my people to action."

"That's the way of the Eyrie," Hafryn muttered with a sigh.

"Indeed," Viren said, eyes amused.

The servers came with steaming plates of meat on beds of greens artfully arranged like rolling hills. As before, guests waited for Sonnen to take the first bite before starting on their meals.

Viren turned his wine glass upside down when a servant came to refill it. He scrutinised Hafryn with piercing intensity. "I've had few reports of you interacting with our brethren in recent seasons, cousin. Tell me, when was the last time you underwent the rites?"

Hafryn hesitated, fork halfway to his lips. "A while, cousin," he conceded.

Danil resisted the urge to frown, unfamiliar with any Eyrie rituals or rites.

"Ah," Viren said, his voice softly chiding. "That must be remedied immediately. I expect you in the training salle in two days hence. One must always respect the traditions of their House."

"It'd be my honor," Hafryn muttered, though nothing in his voice said he meant it.

Viren merely inclined his head.

Gently clearing her throat, Tresa turned back to Danil. "I am told you were born on the deadlands, custodian."

He nodded. "Farin, actually. It was a village on the edge of the deadlands."

"Was?" Tresa tilted her head curiously.

Danil looked up. Her expression appeared disingenuous, but he suspected otherwise. "My people were slaughtered by the magi, my lady. At the time we believed the magi were working on their own, but later discovered that they acted on the orders of King Liam."

"The Roldaerian king, ordering the slaughter of his own people." Tresa shook her head. "It's difficult to fathom."

By instinct, Danil's gaze slid to Viren, whose green eyes sparkled with amusement.

"It shows the depths King Liam will go to gain control of kiandrite crystals," Hafryn pointed out. "What do you think he will do to our people, should his armies reach Amas?"

A flash of irritation showed on Tresa's face. "That is a discussion for the High Council, Hafryn of Eyrie. We're fortunate to have Emissary Arlyn to treat with. It's my hope we can reach some sort of accord."

Danil pushed down his dismay. The only accord the magi of Roldaer would ever agree to was complete ownership of the kiandrite they needed for their spells and curses. The magi would ravage the deadlands to get it, before turning their hunger on Amas.

Tresa seemed willing to ignore such a reality, her face a cool mask as she returned to her plate.

Danil felt little appetite for the remainder of the meal.

10
***

Late evening saw Danil and Hafryn make their way along a corridor lit by iridescent seams of kiandrite. A breeze drifted in from the high windows overhead, where a waxing moon and slow moving clouds were visible. Weariness settled in Danil's bones. He was unused to the wordplay the Amasians seemed to enjoy.

"Is it always like that?" he asked, resisting the urge to fold his arms.

"High stakes? Yes," Hafryn replied grimly. Faint shadows showed under his eyes.

They entered a new corridor where the floor was polished marble. Guards bearing the glyph of Corros on their breast stood at attention in the alcoves and the balcony that opened up to the valley below. Two more guarded a wide oak door.

Hafryn rapped his knuckles on the wood and then pushed his way inside.

Sonnen sat on a plush chair opposite a crackling fire. An aging woman perched on a couch beside him, her bare feet on the thick woven rug. Her white hair was a wild mess about her head, tamed back by a band of tooled leather. Her dark, heavily seamed face reminded Danil of the former healer of Farin, Vellum, who'd had a quick laugh and steady hands.

Beyond the sitting room, the space stretched out into a cavernous, vaulted room with multiple arched doorways, each framed with interwoven glyphs. The far side of the cavern was open to the night sky. The polished floor abruptly dropped away into the inky blackness, and Danil imagined Sonnen in dragon form perched on the ledge before taking flight.

Hafryn paused in front of Sonnen, his arms folded. "What game are you playing at, dragon?" he growled.

Startled, Danil only then noticed the tense line of his friend's back and shoulders.

Sonnen sighed. "Please forgive their intrusion, Freyna," he said to the elderly woman.

The woman, Freyna, looked amused as she tucked her bare feet under her on the couch. "No need," she said, her voice a warm rasp. "It has been too long, my friend."

Contrite, Hafryn bent to press a kiss to her cheek. "Apologies, honored one. It's good to see you."

"And you, little wolf. Sonnen warned you would burst in here like a wildling," she chuckled as she patted his cheek fondly.

Hafryn threw Sonnen a flat look but smiled at Freyna. "May I present you Danil, custodian of the deadlands."

She rose, her simple robes falling about her like water. Smiling, she extended both hands to Danil.

Startled by the gesture, Danil clasped her hands.

"I give you welcome, honored custodian," she said, her dark eyes warm. "I am Freyna, custodian of Corros."

"Oh," Danil said. The crystal grew warm against his chest. "Blessings to your House, Custodian Freyna."

"Such wonderful manners," she chuckled. "But let's not stand on airs. You are Danil, and I Freyna. We're equals, no?"

He smiled. "An exaggeration, but I appreciate it, Freyna."

"Oh, I suspect we shall get on well," Freyna said. She squeezed his hands. "Did you know the deadlands were once called Kailon? A much better name, wouldn't you say?"

"It is," he managed, feeling a sudden sense of rightness in the name. The first crystal warmed on his chest in agreement.

She smiled before turning to Hafryn. "And you, my dear wolf. There is something else different about you. Courtesy of this young man, I suspect."

Hafryn flushed, scrubbing the back of his head. "You always see too much."

"But less than I should," she said, with a momentary flare of regret in her eyes. She drew close and pressed her forehead against Hafryn's for a moment before stepping away. "We shall talk at length, my friend. But another time." Her mirthful eyes slid to Sonnen. "It appears Sonnen has been keeping secrets."

The dragon prince twitched as if fighting the urge to fold his arms. Danil wondered if he'd ever seen him so discomfited before. Sonnen motioned for Danil and Hafryn to sit.

Hafryn remained on his feet. "You could have warned me the Eyrie would be here, Sonnen. With Viren, no less."

Freyna sat back on the couch, curling her feet up under her once more. She leaned on one armrest, chin in her hand to watch the proceedings.

The firelight reflected in Sonnen's golden eyes. "I could have warned you," he agreed.

Hafryn threw up his hands in disgust. He paced the polished floor. "You know Viren will cause trouble."

"It would not have altered your course, in any case," Sonnen said.

"Who is Viren?" Danil asked. "He called Hafryn cousin."

Hafryn folded his arms. "Viren was the one who ordered my exile."

Mouth falling open, Danil said, "Your *cousin* exiled you?"

"Viren was head of the home guard in my village," Hafryn explained, agitation evident in his voice. "The rules are strict. Anyone who reveals their Trueform is of no use to the House. The Eyrie love their secrets. I forced his hand."

"You were a child," Danil argued, appalled.

"Hence exile, and not death," Hafryn pointed out.

Danil was entirely sure that Amasian ways would always remain strange to him.

His expression must have betrayed him, for Sonnen shook his head. "Our peoples are not so different, Danil. You were a child when your village first sent you into the deadlands—into Kailon," he amended. "A place so dangerous that many before you have died."

It was a fair point. Danil settled on the couch beside Freyna.

"It is the focus on our differences that has led us here," Sonnen added. "We must look past them if we are to convince the High Council that Kailon is critical to our future."

Hafryn scowled. "Speaking of. What game is Tresa playing at? She's your representative, but she seemed to accuse Danil of not being a true custodian."

Sonnen frowned. "She knows her task, but many in

Corros are concerned by what it means to have a human custodian." He turned to Freyna. "You might have some insight into this, Freyna, since you became the custodian of Corros when you belonged to another House."

"It indeed took a time for your dam to forgive such a transgression," Freyna said dryly. She gave Danil a measuring look. "But there are tricks we custodians can share."

"I'm not really sure what I'm doing," Danil admitted.

Freyna tilted her head. "You've been under the tutelage of Elania of Corros, have you not?"

"And Blutark," Danil said, surprised at her knowledge.

"Then I'm sure you are further along than you realize. Elania is a most gifted enchanter. They both are."

Danil nodded, though the tight ball in his belly failed to ease.

Freyna took his hand, turning it palm up to trace the glyph. "This says we're of the same House, Danil. But that will not always be so." She closed his hand into a fist. "You're the first custodian of Kailon. There is no path laid out before you."

"I have to make it myself," Danil surmised. He swallowed against the lump in his throat.

Freyna smiled. "That doesn't mean I can't advise you." Her gaze settled on the crystal on Danil's chest. "Walking the leylines is part of who we are as custodians. We show them the safe places where kiandrite can grow, and herd them from places that can cause harm."

Danil thought of the new trees and undergrowth running through Kailon. "The lodestones Kaul stole during the Great War—they come from forested lands, don't they?"

"The Eyrie, mostly, and some from Altonas and Eliar before Kaul poisoned them," Freyna agreed. "Eyrie lands are heavy with rivers and canyons. It's hardly a surprise that their ancient leylines now thrive in Kailon and shape it to resemble their former homeland."

Frowning, Danil asked, "I'd have thought the Eyrie would care what happens in Kailon, then."

Freyna shook her head. "New leylines have grown in Eyrie, though they're strange and at times unwelcoming. No doubt a relic of Kaul's misdeeds. Most Houses carry burdens from the war."

"You mean like what happened to Kailon?" Danil asked.

Sonnen said, "Kailon bore the physical brunt of the war, but many Houses lost glyphs unique to them."

Danil's eyes narrowed. "What do you mean, 'lost'?"

"They disappeared," Hafryn said with a shrug. "All references faded from books and stones, and our enchanters could no longer remember how to create them—not even the commonly used glyphs."

"Sounds like a magi curse," Danil muttered.

"Kaul was half human," Sonnen allowed. "But it is believed he intended neither the breaking of Kailon nor the destruction of our glyphs."

"Really?" Danil asked dubiously. "He was an enemy to Amas. It would make sense he would seek to find a way to destroy your glyphs to ensure his success."

"Quite. And yet the power required to do so would have surely destroyed him long before he was able to lay Kailon to waste. He simply did not have that power," Sonnen said.

Danil nodded in thought. He turned to eye Hafryn. "And what about you? What's this rite that Viren wants you to do?"

Hafryn gave a put-upon sigh. "It's a cleansing. A ritual that Eyrie must partake in if they have been gone from our lands for a time."

"But you're exiled."

"Aye, but I'm still of the House of Eyrie." Hafryn tapped the glyph on the inside of his elbow. "This says I'm bound by certain customs and rituals. I can't ignore Viren's demands, not without gaining a contract on my head."

Sonnen rubbed his chin. "It has been a long time since Viren took an interest in you. There are advantages to acceding to his demands, beyond avoiding your own death of course."

Freyna tilted her head at Sonnen. "You expect Hafryn to find out who purchased the assassin's contract."

Danil raised an eyebrow. "I thought we were keeping that secret."

"From the Roldaerians, yes," Sonnen said. "Freyna is another matter. One does not easily hide such knowledge from his custodian."

"Indeed not," Freyna said with a small smile. She straightened. "Hafryn, is this rite an opportunity to discover Danil's attacker?"

Hafryn shook his head. "Contracts are sworn to secrecy. It's possible the only people who knew of the contact was the assassin, her Keeper and the one who paid for it."

"Who is the Keeper in Corros?" Danil asked.

"As the member of the High Council, it's Viren," Hafryn said. "Although I can't say who was Keeper before he arrived for the meetings. And obviously, we have no way of knowing who among the Eyrie are owl assassins."

Danil bit his lip, debating whether to speak of what he'd seen in the dining hall.

Sonnen appeared unsatisfied. "I want you to begin your search for the one behind the assassin's contract tomorrow, Hafryn. And be cautious should you come upon the Eyrie."

"Aren't I always?"

Sonnen gave him a flat look. "Danil, I'd like you to spend the day with me. I have assurances that there will be no council meetings—official or otherwise. It will serve us well should we happen to bump into councilors during a tour of the citadel. After the display Amaranth's crystal put on this evening, I'm certain that we will have many curious eyes."

"Corros intrigue at its finest," Hafryn said dourly with a shake of his head.

Danil wasn't confident he had the skill for such subtle work, but he nonetheless nodded gamely.

"Excellent. Let's see if we can win ourselves some more votes," Sonnen said.

11

"Emissary Arlyn invites you to breakfast with her, Custodian Danil," a servant said as she stood in the reception room of Hafryn's quarters.

Seated on the couch, Danil hesitated in pulling on his boots. "Oh, I—"

Hafryn strolled out from the bathing pool in a loose robe, toweling his damp hair. "Please inform the emissary that the custodian has other commitments this morning." Hafryn threw himself down on the couch beside Danil, the move exposing his bare chest and belly. He gave the servant a playful wink.

Heat flooded Danil's cheeks.

"Of course, sir. I shall express the sentiment," the servant said, grinning as she bowed. The door closed behind her with a quiet snick.

Eyeing Hafryn's casual dress, Danil said, "Really?"

Hafryn shrugged, grinning. "Anything that avoids the Roldaerians is to our benefit, no?"

"I didn't think we need an excuse."

Hafryn wrapped his finger about the loose lacings of

Danil's tunic. "Hmm, you're right about that, *fala*." His green eyes turned mischievous. "Alas, Sonnen has already claimed you for the day." He lifted himself off the couch.

Sighing, Danil finished pulling on his boots. "Will you be joining us?"

"For a tour of Corros?" Hafryn wrinkled his nose. "There's little new for me to see I'm afraid. Besides, there's the matter of your would-be assassin. Whoever is behind it must be feeling nervous by now."

"If they're in Corros."

Hafryn nodded. "I'll ask around, see if anyone's complaining about a missing servant or stablehand. We might at least discover who our assassin was pretending to be."

"Be careful," Danil said.

Grinning, Hafryn said, "Naturally." He shucked off his robe, hopping on one foot as he pulled on his breeches. "And truly, *fala*, stay clear of the Roldaerians. It wasn't happenstance that Arlyn was seated far from you last night. Sonnen doesn't want anyone to associate you and Roldaer together."

"We're *not* together," Danil growled.

Hafryn tied the lacings of his breeches closed. "I know that, but the High Council may not."

Danil cursed softly under his breath.

"And avoid walking the halls alone, if you can. It would be mightily inconvenient if you came upon whoever sent that owl. If their pockets are deep, they may well send another."

"Well, you can discount Viren as being an assassin," Danil muttered, recalling how the councilor's Trueform had seemed to strip him bare.

"*What?*" Hafryn gaped in astonishment.

Danil said, "Viren's a wolf. Huge, though. Twice the size of your Trueform."

"A Great Wolf," he murmured, looking slightly nervous. "No less dangerous than an owl, but for other reasons." He scrubbed his chin. "I have always wondered about that man." Hafryn looked earnestly at Danil. "Speak of it to no one, Danil. If he has the slightest inkling, the consequences will be catastrophic."

"I swear," Danil said.

A knock on the door had Hafryn moving. Sonnen entered wearing plain grey robes cinched at the waist with a leather belt dotted with kiandrite crystals. The crystal about Danil's neck sang in the back of his mind as if in greeting.

"Am I too early?" Sonnen asked. He eyed Hafryn in amusement as the wolf strode into their sleeping quarters in search of a tunic.

"You're always welcome, Sonnen," Hafryn called out. Pulling the tunic over his head, he added, "Danil and I were just discussing allies."

Sonnen raised an eyebrow. "They aren't always easy to see, especially when the High Council is at play," he agreed. He smiled at Danil. "But you have an ally in the citadel itself, Danil."

"I do?" Danil asked in surprise.

"It's easier if I show you," Sonnen said.

Hafryn finished lacing his tunic. "I'll be down at the harbor if you've need of me."

Sonnen nodded, then waited for Danil to join him.

Outside, they strode along a causeway that led them across the windy battlements and into a second tower. A stairwell took them up a few levels.

Giggling children drew Danil up short. The stairwell opened onto an exposed landing bereft of a roof or walls.

Gleaming tiles of blue and gold covered the floor in a series of intricate circles. Groups of children, some hardly old enough to be out of swaddling cloths, sat in a ring surrounding large glyphs etched into the stone. A youngling stood in the center of each circle, flicking between human and woodland creatures like squirrels, badgers and even an elk. An older shifter, wearing robes of the Corros enchanters, watched over each group, offering advice and encouragement.

"What is this place?" Danil asked in quiet awe.

"Younglings who are new to transformation come here to practice," Sonnen said, watching over the groups. "Transformation can be a difficult experience, especially if the youngling is frightened or unprepared. They can practice here without fear of being injured or hurting others."

Danil watched a girl perhaps twelve summers old flit between human and badger. The children sitting around the circle applauded when she fluidly transformed back.

Sonnen took him on a winding path between the glyph circles. The air took on a low hum as they neared a stretch of floor heavily veined with kiandrite. Glyphs marked the ground here as well but were worn thin and almost invisible in places as if eroded with age.

Sonnen motioned for Danil to kneel beside a vein of kiandrite as thick as his forearm. It startled Danil a little that such wealth could be left unharvested. With a rush of understanding, he realized the Amasians valued kiandrite far more than merely as crystals that powered their enchantments.

"What are we doing here, Sonnen?" Danil asked as he settled on the cool floor.

"People saw how the statue of Aramanth greeted you

last night," Sonnen said. He remained standing, his gaze sweeping over the platform. "It is important that more folk understand your connection to Corros and Amas."

Following his gaze, it took Danil a moment to recognize Freyna seated on a bench on the opposite end of the training circles. A handful of older enchanters milled about her, while Viren sat at her side together with a middle-aged woman bearing an unfamiliar House glyph on her robe. The woman gave Freyna a sapling in a conical pot, her voice too distant to make out.

For his part, Viren appeared attentive to the conversation, but his ghostlike Trueform trotted toward Danil with alarming resolve.

"Place your hand on the kiandrite, Danil."

Blinking his sight clear, Danil said, "Beg pardon?"

Sonnen's golden eyes were unreadable. "It connects directly to the great lodestone of Corros, and cares little for enchanters or human mages," he murmured. "Custodians are another matter."

Danil took in a nearby training circle, where an enchanter watched with folded arms. She seemed not to notice the young boy behind her shifting into a pheasant and back again.

"It's because some people think I can't possibly be a custodian, right?" Danil asked, squinting up at Sonnen.

The dragon prince grunted. "Not everyone, but such people aren't necessarily the ones who matter—not when it comes to Kailon."

A slow anger built in Danil's belly. Kailon was at risk, but he had to somehow prove his legitimacy.

Golden eyes fell on Danil. "What will you do to convince them, Custodian Danil?"

Anything, Danil thought. He set a hand on the vein. The

kiandrite pulsed, turning gold to match the glyph on his palm. A flood of whispers filled his mind, together with an image of a immense crystal seated within a circular stone room. The whispers grew to a roar like wildfire in a forest. A still pool of water formed in his mind's eye. Ash floated in the air above it, speckled with kiandrite turned red and foul.

Danil wrenched his hand back. His lungs burned as if he'd inhaled smoke.

The kiandrite vein flooded with light and released a hum so deep that it vibrated through the floor.

A yelp and the shattering of pottery rang out from the far side of the platform. A wide-leafed plant, six feet tall and with sprawling roots, stood where the sapling had been. Younglings and their enchanter teachers gaped, but Freyna remained seated and appeared wholly unsurprised. Sonnen smirked happily.

"Come here, Danil of Kailon," Freyna called out.

Rising to his feet, Danil nervously wiped his hands on his breeches. He walked between the training circles to where Freyna sat. "Apologies, custodian," he said, feeling eyes on him. "I may have broken your plant."

Freyna's dark eyes were filled with mirth. "Hardly that, my fellow custodian! You've made the gift from Councilor Liria even more princely."

Startled, Danil wondered which House the middle-aged woman represented. She returned his gaze with a mixture of curiosity and caution.

"Of course, I'll need help now to carry my gift to my personal grove," Freyna added with a wink.

"I'd be happy to," Danil stammered, flushing slightly.

Viren stepped forward and gave a smooth bow. "I offer my services as well, Custodian Freyna."

Eyebrow crooked, Freyna glanced up at Sonnen. The

dragon prince looked thoughtful before he nodded. Freyna beamed. "You're most kind, Councilor," she said. She motioned to a nearby enchanter, who magicked a large square of burlap. Danil helped move the plant with its delicate roots into the makeshift carrying sack.

"I'll join you shortly," Sonnen said when Danil was done, turning to speak to Freyna.

Clearly a dismissal, Danil joined Viren in hefting the plant and carrying it off the platform. They navigated the stairwell, pausing at the edge of a causeway.

"I don't know the way to the grove," Danil admitted.

"And I don't give a damn about an overgrown weed," Viren said dryly. He set down his side, forcing Danil to release the plant as well.

The Eyrie councilor studied him with green eyes so like Hafryn's that Danil felt a moment of disorientation. He resisted the urge to step back.

"Parlor tricks might turn a few heads, human, but you'll need to do something more substantial to secure the High Council's aid."

Danil blinked. "Beg pardon?"

"Being a custodian is not enough." Viren eyed him critically. "I'd expected you to be better prepared."

"I handled things well in Kailon," Danil countered. He wondered if Viren knew of the Eyrie assassin after all.

Viren sniffed. "Perhaps so, but your helpers have failed you here."

He stiffened at that. "Do you mean Sonnen? Or your cousin?"

"I'll get a measure of Hafryn during the rites tomorrow." Viren smiled slightly. "But you, custodian—if you wish the High Council to be on your side, you'd best present a more inviting offer than the Roldaerian emissary."

"And I suppose you already know what Arlyn is after," Danil muttered.

"You flew in with her—I'd hoped Hafryn at least would have taken advantage of that time to glean her terms."

Danil scowled.

Viren shook his head in disappointment. "Not everyone on the High Council wants to treat with Roldaer, but the alternative isn't particularly...inspiring. Leylines notwithstanding, no House wants to send their people to die on a ruined tract of land that is better left forgotten to our darkest histories."

Gritting his teeth, Danil said, "Thank you for making your stance clear."

"Don't presume to know the Eyrie, human. That will be your last mistake."

Viren left him there on the causeway. Not even his wolf Trueform looked back.

12

Hafryn returned as night fell over the citadel. Dusty and frowning, his pace slowed at the sight of Danil alone outside, leaning against the balustrade.

A flock of birds circled the neighboring spire, and Danil idly wondered if they were shifters as they wheeled down to the lake far below. He turned from the balcony to study Hafryn.

"Let me guess," Hafryn said, the chill breeze pulling at his cloak. "Your day was as unsuccessful as mine."

"That's a way to describe it," Danil said sourly. Other than the occasional greeting, no Councilor appeared willing to talk to him at length about the future of Kailon. He sighed disconsolately. "No luck in finding who ordered the assassin's contract, then?"

Hafryn shook his head. "I wasn't able to speak to the former Eyrie Keeper—it appears she's parted ways with the folk of Corros."

Danil raised an eyebrow, supposing murder among their own kind wasn't much of a stretch for the Eyrie.

"She's not dead, *fala*," Hafryn said, clearly having read something in Danil's expression. "Just returned to Eyrie."

"How inconvenient," Danil replied with another sigh.

Hafryn gave a huff and waved his hand dismissively. "I'm barely started. There are plenty enough people to badger and bribe. If the clues are here, we'll find them." He settled beside Danil, fingers tapping on the smooth stone. "I'm guessing Sonnen didn't take you much outside of this spire."

Danil nodded. The citadel was far more expansive than he'd expected. Throughout the day, as Sonnen had taken him on a wandering path through the towers, they'd come upon various members of the High Council. Most were polite, almost painfully so while under Sonnen's eye. But Danil couldn't help but wonder how many were allies he could count upon to protect Kailon.

"The High Council were—" Danil struggled for the words. "Difficult to impress."

Hafryn snorted. "No surprise there, *fala*. They perch so high up in their towers that they forget what it means to actually have to fight for anything important." He studied Danil's bleak profile. "Let's not worry about the High Council tonight, hmn? There's a place I think you'd enjoy."

Weary and a little despondent, Danil nonetheless nodded.

Hafryn took him on a wandering course down to a lower keep, where its roof was flat but lined with battlements. Amasians took their ease in the cool night air, with a handful of vendors selling cooked meats and pockets of bread stuffed with pickled vegetables and spices.

To Danil's surprise, a number of Amasians waved or smiled in greeting.

"Custodian."

"Bright evening to you both," another said as she strolled past.

Danil noticed folk wearing enchanter robes milling amongst the crowd. They nodded to him in greeting. No one appeared finely dressed, with laborers and guards mixing with younglings and families. Danil's vision shifted to reveal a variety of ghostly Trueforms gamboling, lounging and prancing across the rooftop.

He turned about in a slow circle. This was what he'd expected to find in Corros—not the stiff neutrality of councilors and elites.

A young girl abruptly ran up to Danil and snared his arm. "You're him!" she breathed, her blue eyes dancing. A little blackbird Trueform flitting excitedly in the air above her. "Mama, he made the verisa tree in the training grounds grow a hundred feet tall!"

Hafryn raised an amused eyebrow as Danil stammered and flushed.

"Oh, no, I—"

A woman with blond hair bound in twin braids came to fetch the girl. "Leave off with him, Perena. Let the custodian have some peace."

"She's no trouble," Danil said to the woman.

Perena beamed up at him. "I'm going to be an enchanter. Mama says you don't have many in Kailon and need all the help you can get!"

"Perena!" the woman hissed, cheeks reddening.

Danil crouched until he was eye level with the young girl. "Sadly, your mama has the right of it, but some of my greatest friends are enchanters—they're among the bravest and most loyal people I know."

Perena nodded as if it was no surprise.

"Together, we are doing the best we can to protect the

new leylines in Kailon. I'm sure you'll make a great enchanter one day," Danil added. "When you are older and trained and have your mother's permission, of course, I'd more than welcome your aid in protecting Kailon."

She squealed with delight and wrapped her arms around his neck. "I will," she promised. "Mama says it's a great honor to serve a first custodian." Glancing at him and Hafryn, she asked with excited eyes, "Will you light the lanterns with us?"

Danil threw a confused look at Hafryn.

"It's a nightly practice here in Corros," Hafryn explained. "Enchanters each release a magelight, while those of us without such gifts or aren't proficient yet—" He gave Perena a wink. "Fire off our own lantern. It signifies that we all have a place in Corros."

A sudden lump grew in Danil's throat at the thought of such easy belonging. "It sounds wonderful," he managed as he smiled down at the girl.

Perena brightened again as she tugged his hand. "This way! You can use my brother's lantern. He's working in the kitchens tonight." She peered at Hafryn following bemusedly behind them with the girl's mother and wavered. "You can have mine, if you like."

Hafryn pressed a hand to his heart and bowed. "You're most generous, little enchanter, but if it's alright, Danil and I might share."

The young girl shrugged in agreement. She reached a blanket stretched out on the roof, where a man of a similar age to Hafryn sat with a baby heavily wrapped in swaddling cloths. With an easy smile, the man handed Danil a small square of blue paper.

"Bright evening to you, custodian," the man nodded respectfully.

"And to you," Danil replied.

"Here," Hafryn said, showing how to open the lantern. There was a faint iridescent sheen to the paper. "Fire will activate it. Ah—right on time."

Danil turned to see Freyna walk amidst the crowd. Plainly dressed in a grey robe and her white hair free about her face, she fit well amongst the gathering. In her cupped hands sat a tiny flame. As she passed, Amasians dipped their paper lanterns into the fire before hurtling them skywards. They caught alight with a soft 'puff' before transforming into showers of brightly colored light that fell harmlessly over the rooftop and onto the surrounding spires.

Enchanters released magelights into the air to dance and whizz about the burning lanterns. Similar showers of light came from the surrounding towers.

"Your lanterns, if you please."

Danil startled to see Freyna paused in front of him.

The custodian smiled, the lines about her eyes crinkling. She lowered her hands to allow Perena easy access to the flame. With a delighted squeal, the girl took off running, the burning lantern held aloft as it shot out sparks across the roof.

"It won't cause burns," Hafryn said, watching the young girl with amusement. "Great for pranks, though."

"Of which you have yet to grow out of," Freyna observed, though her voice was fond.

Danil's gaze caught on a particularly bright shower of hot pink and orange as it burst overhead. "You do this every night?"

"It's one of my great pleasures," Freyna said. She held the flame aloft. "Light your lantern, Danil of Kailon. Tomorrow, we shall talk."

Swallowing, Danil tilted the blue paper into the fire. The edge caught, and he handed it to Hafryn. With a grin, Hafryn hurled it into the air. A few heartbeats later, it burst into streamers of gold and red. A magelight buzzed around the changing lights before flitting off.

Smiling, Freyna said, "Enjoy your night." She melted back into the crowd, leaving bursts of light and laughter in her wake.

Danil and Hafryn settled onto the shared blanket as more Amasians took seats around them and watched the bursting lanterns long into the night.

13

The following morning, Danil woke to Hafryn climbing across the fur pallet. Half asleep, he grabbed a handful of tunic and tugged the shifter close. His mouth found the soft underside of Hafryn's throat.

Hafryn chuckled in his ear. "Tempting, *fala*, but we have company."

That woke him fully. Danil peered over Hafryn's shoulder to the partition leading into the central living space. He saw a pair of small, woman-sized boots. He flailed. "Off, off," he whispered, whacking Hafryn's shoulder.

The wolf shifter obligingly rose onto one elbow, green eyes bright with amusement. "She's here for you."

Danil rolled off the pallet and hurriedly grabbed his tunic. "You couldn't have woken me sooner?" he hissed.

"I enjoy you in my bed, *fala*," Hafryn said, unabashedly watching as Danil struggled into his breeches. The wolf shifter was already fully dressed, boots and all.

With a snort, Danil tucked his crystal under his tunic before leaning in to plant his mouth over Hafryn's. He pulled back to see the shifter's eyes drift shut. "You'll be safe today, yes?"

"Hmm, you have my word the ritual's nothing I haven't experienced before," Hafryn said. He sprawled back across the furs, his hands tucked behind his head.

Danil eyed him. "That's hardly reassuring—I know you, wolf."

"It appears so." Hafryn schooled his face to innocence. "I might learn something of interest today. That's far more important, in my opinion."

With a sigh, Danil asked, "Come find me when you're done?"

"Of course."

Danil entered the living quarters to see Freyna comfortably seated on the couch by the fire. He sketched a quick bow. "I apologize for the wait, honored custodian."

"These old bones demand I sleep less than I should." She rose with a smile. "And youth has its own demands."

Dani fought not to blush. "Yes, honored custodian."

"Freyna, Danil, as we agreed."

"Yes, Freyna."

"I understand you have seen a little of our great citadel. Considering events over the past few days, we shall visit a few of my favored places."

Danil smiled. "I'd like that."

They stepped out into the hallway before taking windings steps cut into the cliff. The valley spread out below them, with waterfalls a dull roar in the distance. Cloud hung low over the peaks, and Danil's gaze turned instinctively east toward the deadlands. He could sense the leylines contentedly pulsing under his skin.

"You called the deadlands Kailon," Danil said. "Does that mean something?"

Freyna ran her hand along the railing. "It's an old Amasian word. Loosely translated, it means 'to stand between,'" she said, her dark eyes studying the peaks. "Before the Great War, it had been the trading hub between our two kingdoms."

Danil sensed again the pull of the leylines and felt a sudden yearning. "What happened to its custodian? During the war, I mean?"

The bottom of the stairs opened onto a small platform.

"You are Kailon's first custodian, Danil. There were no leylines to speak of running through the area, not before Kaul played his part in making the wellspring." Freyna shook her head. "It gives reason to so much disquiet among the High Council. Leylines have formed where they should not, under land made dead and quiet. And now they are busily reforming that land, under the guidance of a young human. People are uncertain."

"Are you?" Danil asked before he could stop himself.

She smiled, the seams about her eyes deepening. "I can feel the strength in your leylines, Danil. That is cause for celebration, not apprehension."

The tension refused to leave his shoulders. "I'm guessing there aren't many on the High Council who like humans."

Freyna waved it aside as they entered a dark and cool corridor. Guards stood at attention at random intervals, and Danil wondered what they protected.

"You're hardly the first human to walk these halls, Danil," Freyna said. "Our quarrel lies with Roldaer, not humanity. And yes, I'm aware of your story. Sonnen has shared your exploits with the High Council—I won't lie and say that your Roldaerian heritage doesn't matter, but your deeds speak well of you. And let's not forget that Kailon's leylines trust your judgment. Otherwise, they would never have chosen you."

"I don't think they had many other options," Danil admitted, recalling the desperate fight in the temple.

Freyna scoffed. "Custodians aren't chosen by happenstance. The wellspring called you to it, no?"

Hesitating, Danil nodded.

"It was no different for me," Freyna said. "I was part of a trade delegation from Jolun House, and on my first night, I found myself wandering the halls until I came upon the great lodestone. Despite coming from another House, no one cast doubt over my legitimacy as the future custodian of Corros."

Danil knew he didn't have that luxury. "Arlyn meets with the High Council today," he said with trepidation. Despite her consistently warm demeanor, Danil could not believe that her intentions toward Kailon were benevolent.

"And you'll have your turn soon enough." She patted his arm gently. "Trust that the people of Amas will not let Kailon fall to ruin again."

Danil hoped that she was right.

An innocuous wooden door lead into a small chamber. At its center stood a massive crystal taller than Danil and just as broad. It glowed a mellow, deep blue with dots of light that swirled and danced as if in a breeze.

"The first crystal of Corros," Freyna said, her voice reverent.

"It's magnificent," Danil breathed. Against his chest, his crystal turned a surly yellow that leaked through his tunic. By habit, Danil gripped it and admired its steady warmth. *'You're still my favorite,'* he thought, fighting down his amusement.

The crystal brightened to gold.

Freyna looked bemused. "Your kiandrite is most responsive," she said. "Wherever did you come upon it?"

Danil smiled. "It was a gift," he said, thinking of the leylines.

"It will certainly serve you well. We custodians have a unique connection with kiandrite that manifests in unexpected ways."

Danil watched the custodian circle the giant crystal.

"How did it get so big?"

"As a first crystal, it chooses its own shape based on the needs of the leylines." She gave the crystal a cheeky smile. "It has grown fat and spoiled under my care, I'm afraid."

The first crystal flushed with affronted pink, and Freyna laughed.

"I like you this way, old friend. It means that the leylines are safe, and so is Amas." Her smile dimmed, and a small frown appeared on her brow. "I fear the time is fast approaching when that will no longer be the case, and we will need your steely heart once more."

The crystal darkened in agreement, and Danil felt an odd sensation on his chest as his own crystal responded. It felt like an agreement was made between the two powerful pieces of kiandrite, and Danil felt inexplicably relieved.

Freyna looked at the two crystals curiously but didn't comment. She stepped away from the crystal. "Come, there is another chamber I would show you."

A small alcove lead into an antechamber. It was compact and perfectly circular, but Danil's attention was snared by the towering height of the walls. They sprawled upwards like a chimney, so high that Danil caught sight of a dot of blue sky. He turned about in a slow circle. Flecks of kiandrite sparkled in the rocks. But what caught Danil's attention was the array of glyphs that spanned the height of the chimney. No two glyphs were the same.

"What is this place?" Danil asked.

Freyna clasped her hands behind her back and looked up. "The catacombs here hold every glyph that has ever been used in Corros."

It startled Danil out of his reverie. "*All* of them?"

"What is left of them, in any case," Freyna said, staring up at the countless winking lights. "The great lodestone sits below this very chamber, and it has a thirst for the knowledge the glyphs bring. Many enchanters throughout Amas come to Corros to learn from them."

Danil noticed a small handful of glyphs upon the ground. He respectfully sidestepped around each one as he inspected those closest on the wall.

"What is it that you see, custodian?" she asked intently.

He turned back to Freyna, startled to see a ghostly wren perched upon her shoulder. Her Trueform would have been unremarkable, save for the iridescent lines of kiandrite threading through her wings. He rubbed his eyes, but the wren remained visible.

"The floor, Danil," Freyna pressed.

Danil frowned, glancing down. "Do you mean the glyphs?"

Her eyes widened slightly. "I knew it," she breathed.

He turned to fully face her.

"The protective glyphs ensure none may enter who would steal or damage the catacombs," Freyna said. "They are visible to no one—and with good reason. How many do you see?"

Danil did a quick count. "Twelve."

"To match the twelve Houses of Amas," she breathed. Freyna suddenly hugged him. "Oh, what a mysterious gift you are, Danil! The High Council must know. It changes everything!"

"I-I don't know what you mean," Danil said.

Freyna pulled back, beaming. "We may have found a way save Kailon."

14

T hey came upon Hafryn limping along a corridor a short time later. To Danil's surprise, the wolf shifter was being half-supported by Griff, who bore a dour expression as he eased Hafryn down onto a bench seat outside a meeting hall.

"What happened?" Danil asked in alarm.

"*Fala!*" Hafryn gave him a sloppy grin. A cut showed above his hairline.

Griff looked relieved to hand the wolf over. "Found him wandering outside the training halls. Says he's finished his cleansing."

The wolf's eyes were distinctly unfocused.

"He's badly hurt," Danil growled. "We have to get him to the healers."

The blue dragon shrugged. "He mentioned something about ephril."

Freyna muttered something under her breath. "It's a curative the Eyrie use to muddle the mind," she explained to Danil.

"Had to take it," Hafryn argued, attempting to straighten.

"It's part of the ritual. Take the ephril, then do battle." He blinked, his eyes focusing on Danil. "Hello, *fala*." He reached out as if to draw him close.

Danil steadied him. "How long will the effects last?"

"A half day or so, by all reports," Freyna said. "It creates hallucinations. The Eyrie use it in cleansing battles so that the supplicant is never quite sure what Trueform they fought against."

"No owls," Hafryn mumbled. "Big wolf, though." He frowned muzzily at the ceiling. "Maybe it was my own wolf."

Freyna sighed. "Best you take him to your rooms, Danil. I'll send for a healer." She turned to Griff. "Thank you for aiding our friend. We'll deal with him from here."

Relief showed on the blue dragon's face. He bowed to the custodian before stalking down the corridor.

"Surly," Hafryn muttered, then burped inelegantly. "Not like you, *fala*."

Danil wondered if the injury was worse than first appeared.

Freyna gave a soft chuckle. "Your beloved will be fine, Danil."

"Quietly, honored custodian," Hafryn whispered conspiratorially. He tapped his nose. "He doesn't know the real meaning of *fala*."

Danil resisted a sigh. "Real meaning? Why am I not surprised you lied about it?"

"It's an old Amasian term for beloved." Amusement colored Freyna's voice.

Danil scowled at the wolf. "You told me it meant moonflower."

"At the time, you weren't ready for it to be anything else," Hafryn said with a dismissive sniff.

Freyna's smile widened.

"Gods, let's get you back to our rooms," Danil muttered. He threw Hafryn's arm over his shoulder to steady him.

Freyna's apparent enjoyment of the situation only grew. "Go on with your beloved, Danil. I'll organize a meeting with the High Council—this cannot wait a few days."

"Thank you, honored custodian."

The aging woman gave him a bow and continued along the corridor.

With a sigh, Danil heaved Hafryn upright. "You could have warned me," he muttered.

"About ephril?" Hafryn squinted at him.

"No, the fighting."

Hafryn snorted. "That would have happened no matter what. Better this way. Means the Eyrie don't plan to kill me."

"Really? What makes you so certain?"

"There are rules after the cleansing rites." Hafryn gave him a surreptitious wink. "Two weeks of being untouchable by any of the Eyrie. Viren did us a favor, though I don't know why." He smirked suddenly. "And they barely even got a kick in."

Danil eyed the cut on his friend's forehead. "Right. Come on, then." He hauled Hafryn a few feet along the corridor.

The wolf suddenly paled, wavering on his feet. "I need to sit down a moment," Hafryn said, eyes earnest and face decidedly green.

"You can't make it back to our rooms, can you?"

"Hmm."

With a sigh, Danil hailed a nearby guard to go in search of a healer.

～

THE HEALERS SENT them away at midday with a harsh rebuke about Eyrie tricks and hallucinogens wasting the healer's time. Clear-eyed and amused, Hafryn sketched a bow at the glowering woman before jauntily strolling from the healing hall and into the corridor leading back to their quarters.

Danil trailed after him, noting the stiff line of Hafryn's back. "You didn't tell them about your ribs."

The wolf sniffed, stepping close to the wall to allow a pair of young shifters to pass. "It's nothing to speak of, *fala*."

"Really?" Danil folded his arms. "Like the cleansing rite that caused it?"

Hafryn looked at him sidelong. "The Eyrie have traditions that aren't easy to explain—not even among fellow Amasians."

Danil scowled. "Try me."

Hafryn suddenly noticed the unhappy set of Danil's mouth. "I—not here. I'm sorry, *fala*. The Eyrie isn't the only House with spies."

"Our quarters, then."

"You're stubborn," Hafryn marveled. "Not a surprise, of course, but sometimes I forget the full measure of it."

Danil shifted his feet. "Maybe so, but you forget to trust me, too."

Hafryn frowned. "That's quite a leap, don't you think?"

"Is it? Ever since we got here, you've kept things from me, hidden things." Danil swallowed heavily. "You've lied to me, Hafryn."

Hafryn's mouth fell open before he shut it with a click. "It's not for the reasons you think." He gave a humorless grimace. "You've your own issues to deal with. I didn't want to burden you with family squabbles as well."

Danil's heart did a slow, heavy roll. "We're in this together, aren't we?"

Hafryn blinked and tilted his head, green eyes clearing. "Oh, *fala,* we are indeed. This is yet another transgression I must atone for." He took Danil's hand and kissed the knuckles. "Truly, I—"

The floor suddenly trembled under their feet.

Spinning, Danil watched as seams of kiandrite in the walls flared an angry red before a blood-curdling scream rang out.

"That sounded close," Danil gasped.

"Come on!"

They entered the corridor at a sprint, hurtling past startled shifters to see guards frantically kicking the door to their own rooms. The wood splintered with a crack.

Leaping over the shattered remains of the door, Danil saw a charred body lying amidst the overturned couch and table. A few feet away lay Freyna. Blood pooled under the custodian. A cold bite hung in the air, along with it the strange scent of lightning during a storm. The room was tinged red as the kiandrite continued to glow angrily with harsh bursts of scarlet so dark it occasionally turned black.

Danil quickly turned Freyna over. She was shockingly pale, with blood coating the front of her robe. Her eyes opened a fraction before closing once again.

"She's alive," Hafryn muttered. "Get a healer in here!" he yelled to the guards. One took off at a sprint.

Freyna's breath rattled in her throat.

Danil gripped her hand. "Help's coming, Freyna. Stay with us."

From the corner of his eye, he saw a guardsman bend over the dead man.

"Don't touch him," Hafryn barked even as he pressed a

wad of cloth to Freyna's side. "Even I can sense the death enchantment over him."

Charred blackness scoured away much of the man's flesh, leaving him unrecognizable. Danil's stomach turned. The room smelled like the toxic and blackened fields that covered most of the deadlands.

Suddenly, Sonnen pushed his way into the room. He took a quick look about, his golden eyes flaming, and knelt beside Danil to gently cup Freyna's face. "Custodian," he rumbled.

Freyna's eyes cracked open. Her mouth worked, but no sound came out.

"No, don't speak," Sonnen said. "Reserve your strength, my friend."

She gave out a weak rasp as she clasped his arm. "*Videre.*"

Viren abruptly pushed into the gap between Danil and Sonnen, a woman in brown healer robes on his heels. "Clear a space," the Eyrie councilor ordered tersely.

Danil rose to his feet, watching anxiously as the healer knelt beside Freyna and began her work. Hafryn moved to stand beside him.

Both Sonnen and Viren followed the directions of the healer as she pressed a bandage lined with glyphs to Freyna's side.

"Let's get her to the infirmary," the healer muttered, motioning to the guards. A pair gently eased Freyna up, and in a rush, they vacated the rooms.

A momentary quiet settled over the room. Hafryn scrubbed wet hands through his hair and cursed.

"Stay a moment, Viren," Sonnen growled as the councilor made for the door. The dragon prince wiped blood onto his breeches.

Viren paused beside the destroyed side table, his expression carefully blank.

Sonnen pointed to the charred body. "If you please."

Danil and Hafryn joined them in squatting over the dead man. There was little left to mark the man, the body charred beyond recognition. A dagger remained clenched in one clawed hand, its tip coated in blood.

Sonnen pulled free a scrap of charred fabric under the body and inspected the fine stitching. With a grunt, he handed the material to Hafryn.

"Eyrie cloth," the wolf muttered, tilting it toward the light streaming in from the balcony.

Flames showed bright and raging in Sonnen's eyes as he turned to Viren. "Best you have an explanation, councilor," he growled.

Viren frowned and motioned for Hafryn to hand over the cloth. At Sonnen's nod, the wolf obeyed. A moment passed before Viren set down the fabric. He sighed. "Hafryn is right, though I promise, your highness, there are none among my people who would dare attack the custodian of Corros."

"It is unlikely that she was the intended target," Sonnen muttered, his gaze flicking to Danil.

Viren looked Danil up and down, green eyes bland. "While your human may cause anxiety among the High Council, Prince Sonnen, I can assure you no one has approached me with a contract to...rectify matters."

Danil's skin pebbled under the stony regard.

Viren tilted his head, eyes narrowing. "Why was Freyna here, in any case?" he asked Danil. "You two were last seen together in the catacombs."

Wondering how the councilor knew that, Danil folded his arms. "We parted ways before midday. Last I saw, she was headed for the High Council. I'd hoped to join her but was waylaid when Hafryn needed the healers."

Sonnen's eyes narrowed upon the Eyrie councilor. The man appeared unconcerned.

"Just the effects of ephril," Hafryn muttered to Sonnen.

Danil glowered. "*Not* just the ephril."

The flames in Sonnen's eyes deepened.

"The ritual may have been more vigorous than usual," Viren allowed, straightening. At Sonnen's deepening growl, the councilor sighed and pulled a small vial from his pouch. "This should remedy any lasting effects of Hafryn's cleansing."

Danil took the vial before the wolf could reach for it. He unstoppered the cork and sniffed it suspiciously. "You couldn't have given it to Hafryn earlier?"

The man said nothing, eyes hooded.

"It's not poison, *fala*." Hafryn took the vial and swallowed the contents with a grimace. "Eyrie often refuse healers because they pride themselves on their ability to ignore injury."

"A skill you seem to have lost," Viren noted with a disdainful sniff.

"Aye, without any regret," Hafryn countered, baring his teeth.

Sonnen shook his head. "In any case, the High Council's session with Emissary Arlyn today was shorter than expected. Freyna must have come here when she discovered the chambers were empty."

"What was so important that she went to the High Council?" Viren asked. "I understood she was to be with the human custodian today."

Hafryn tilted his head. "Who else knew that Danil was

spending the day with Freyna? And that I'd likely be waylaid by my...cleansing ceremony?"

Viren stilled, green eyes chill. "What are you implying, cousin?"

"Would any of your underlings take a contract without your knowledge?" Hafryn asked.

"No."

"So certain," Sonnen marveled with a mocking shake of his head.

Viren inclined his head. "I am, my prince. That is the surety of the Eyrie—no unauthorized contracts, no solo missions. Our work is for the wealth of all of Eyrie. We don't freelance."

"So you say, but this assassin was obviously waiting for Danil to return alone or with me incapacitated," Hafryn growled. "He was caught by surprise when it was Freyna he attacked. Hence why instead of the killing blow, the dagger went into her side—he likely changed the direction of the blow the moment he realized his mistake."

"And then the leylines dealt with him," Sonnen stated. "There is a chance the leylines will react similarly if Danil is under threat."

"An interesting theory, my prince," Viren said, green eyes narrow. "But I assure you, none of my people are behind this."

"Is anyone among your retinue missing?" Hafryn asked.

"This man is not one of mine."

"How can you be so sure?" Danil asked. "He's wearing an Eyrie tunic."

Viren waved his hand in dismissal. "Our cloth is available to any with the coin and stupidity to wear it. I assure you, had he crossed paths with one of my people, he would not have survived it."

"No one wears Eyrie cloth but the Eyrie," Hafryn explained to Danil.

Danil raised an eyebrow. "*You* don't wear it."

Hafryn suddenly coughed. "For an entirely different reason, *fala*."

Viren's gaze turned measuring.

"What about before you arrived?" Danil pressed Viren. "There were Eyrie already stationed here in Corros—anyone missing?"

Viren began to shake his head, then paused, a frown flickering across his face.

Sonnen made a low rumble and balled his fists.

The Eyrie leader's expression smoothed over. "Many Eyrie come and go according to the demands of their contracts. I've received no report of note, I'm afraid." He rose, dusting his hands on his breeches. "Now, if you'll excuse me, there are some things I must attend to. Unless I am to be detained."

Sonnen looked sorely tempted. "You are not. But I will have more questions for you, councilor," he growled with such venom that the hackles stood on the back of Danil's neck.

Viren sketched a quick bow. "And I will answer them, my prince." He bowed again and then left without a backward glance.

Hafryn waited a few heartbeats before giving a low whistle. "I think Viren just discovered he has less control over his assassins than he thought."

"That is hardly in our favor," Sonnen growled, golden eyes dark.

15

The furnishings in Sonnen's private guest wing were simple but finely made, the second doorway leading to a balcony that looked out onto the valley below. The sparseness of the room was a sharp contrast to Hafryn's quarters, which were now closed to them while enchanters worked to put it to rights. Danil wasn't entirely sure he wanted to go back there—not when Freyna's life hung in the balance.

"It's temporary until our quarters are dealt with," Hafryn said, throwing his cloak over the back of a chair.

Danil dropped his pack at the end of a sleeping pallet. "It's fine," he said after a time. "I just—I don't understand why I can't join you."

"In hunting down who's trying to kill you?" Hafryn asked. "I'd think it obvious, *fala*." He slipped a dagger into his boot.

Danil resisted the urge to fold his arms. "Were the situation reversed, I'd never expect you to hold back."

Hafryn checked his blade before sliding it into its sheath. "It's not because I don't think you're capable."

"What, then?"

"We can't know what would happen if you're hurt or killed." Hafryn drew close and gripped his shoulders. "Kailon needs its custodian safe."

Danil set his jaw. "Kailon didn't choose me because I take the safest path," he muttered.

Hafryn tightened his grip. "But I need you to do exactly that, Danil. Just this once. I'll be back before dawn," he promised.

Following him into the reception room, Danil watched with a heavy heart as Hafryn joined three shifters waiting by the main door. With a nod, Hafryn led them outside.

The low rumble of Sonnen's voice drifted in from the drawing room, followed by a servant's quiet reply.

At a loss over what to do, Danil loitered in the doorway as the servant departed. Sonnen sat at a large desk of polished wood, his ornate cloak draped over the back of his chair. At some point, the dragon had rolled up his sleeves, a collection of missives spread about him. A frown of concentration marred his forehead as he worked.

The dragon noticed Danil and motioned toward one of the plush chairs on the opposite side of the desk. "Come join me, Danil. You are welcome here."

Danil sat with a murmur of thanks. He waited as Sonnen scrawled upon a length of parchment, the scratch of his quill a loud contrast to the soft crackle of the fire in the hearth. The flames danced merrily, but Danil scarcely felt little beyond a slow chill in his bones.

"Fear not, Danil. Freyna yet lives," Sonnen said, not looking up from his work. "We would know if it were otherwise."

Danil clenched the arms of his chair. "Will she recover?"

Sonnen paused, golden eyes piercing. "What does the kiandrite tell you?"

That startled Danil upright. "Oh, I—" He closed his eyes and mentally reached out, questioning, but felt only an angry buzzing. Even his own crystal felt agitated. "I don't know."

Sonnen tapped a finger on the desk. "I too can sense their outrage, as will anyone with a feel for enchantments. Never before has a custodian been attacked. Not in Corros."

Swallowing, Danil said, "Will the kiandrite keep her alive?"

"Custodians have no right to a longer life than anyone else, no matter how the leylines beneath us demand otherwise. Their interference in the attack is beyond the understanding of what we have always known about them. The leylines provide us with the power for our enchantments, but they do not dictate how we use that gift, nor do they act with a will of their own."

Danil thought of Kailon and suspected otherwise.

Sonnen sat back, his gaze assessing. "It will be interesting to see what happens should Roldaer enter your territory, Danil. The outcome may not be so easy to predict."

Shifting uncomfortably, Danil said, "Emissary Arlyn has already spoken to the High Council."

"A courtesy that would be extended to any kingdom's ambassador."

"She'll leverage the attack on Freyna to her benefit."

Sonnen gave him a studied look. "Not if Hafryn finds a lead. Give it some time. There are a few marketplaces to examine, and many stores, assuming of course that our would-be assassin acquired his outfit here in Corros."

"You don't think so?"

"I take Viren at his word that the Eyrie are not involved in today's attack. That it is Freyna and not you in the infirmary is evidence enough—the Eyrie do not make such mistakes." Sonnen set aside his quill and scrunched the parchment in his fist. It caught alight and quickly turned to ash, replaced by a ball of light. Danil idly watched as the light flew across the room and out the window. "Nonetheless, the citadel is in lockdown. These quarters are out of bounds to all but my closest advisors. You joined my House in good faith, Danil, and I will not flinch from the responsibilities that entails."

"Maybe Kailon would be better off with a different custodian," Danil said, sinking into his chair. "One Amasians don't want to kill."

Sonnen shook his head. "Without you, Kailon will fall to Roldaer—and Amas with it. I have no doubt. You bring change that many find difficult to reconcile, but that is not your fault or your duty to correct." A hard glitter showed in the dragon's eyes.

A hard lump formed in his throat. "It'll all come to nothing if Freyna dies."

"We can only hope she does not."

A polite knock interrupted further conversation.

"Enter," Sonnen commanded.

A servant bowed before stepping aside to grant Councilor Tresa entry. The woman was still dressed in her official robes, her dark hair piled up high above her head once more.

Sonnen rose and gave a short bow, and Danil hastened to follow. "Lady Tresa," the dragon murmured.

"My prince," Tresa replied, pausing on the edge of the rug. "I had hoped to speak to you in private."

"If it regards today's events, then it is best Custodian Danil hears it also," Sonnen said.

Her eyes narrowed. "I see." Tresa inclined her head, causing the blue gems in her hair to sparkle.

"Excellent. Let us share some tea." Sonnen motioned to the servant, who quietly departed the room. "Please, Tresa, sit with us."

She bowed and took the chair a few feet from Danil, her robes rustling as she neatly folded her hands.

They waited in silence for the servant to return with a pot of tea on a small tray. The servant poured three cups, the fragrant scent of spiced oranges filling the air, and handed the first cup to Sonnen.

The dragon murmured his thanks, then indicated for Danil and Tresa to help themselves.

Tresa studied them both over the rim of her cup. "I am told the dagger that struck our honored custodian was not poisoned."

Sonnen nodded. "We are fortunate, indeed."

"Has the perpetrator been identified?"

"My best people are working toward that as we speak," Sonnen replied. "I will be sure to apprise you when we have anything new."

Tresa took a delicate sip. "I understand Hafryn of Eyrie is involved in the search."

The lines about Sonnen's eyes tightened slightly. "You are well informed, Tresa, as always."

"You don't see an issue when the crime took place in his quarters?"

Danil frowned, hearing the implications in her voice.

Sonnen appeared unfazed. "Hafryn is one of our finest trackers. You demanded his skills when we first discovered that kiandrite was entering Kailon through our meltwater," he said. "He has a certain aptitude for finding things that others would prefer hidden."

Tresa took another sip of her tea as her gaze slid to Danil. "And I understand that you are now under guard."

Danil stiffened.

"For his protection," Sonnen clarified with a frown.

The councilor smiled benignly. "Of course. Today's unpleasantness aside, I imagine the reprieve has been welcome."

Danil set down his cup. "Forgive me, councilor, but I'm unsure what you speak of."

"From the deadlands, of course." Her eye widened innocently.

"It is not dead anymore, my lady," Danil said. "And it's called Kailon."

Tresa raised an eyebrow. "According to whom?"

"The histories of our people, Tresa," Sonnen said, annoyance flashing across his face. "We have spoken in depth about what Kailon means to Amas."

"And I've been sure to express the views of Corros to the High Council," Tresa replied. "I'm certain we shall enjoy a desirable outcome. But tell me, Sonnen, can you recall a time when a custodian of Corros was attacked?"

"I cannot."

Her eyes slid back to Danil. "How curious, then, it should occur when and where it did."

Sonnen glowered. "Speak plainly, Tresa."

She set her cup aside and smoothed down her robes. "Very well. This one you call custodian of a dubious scrap of land arrives in Corros, and within days our very own custodian is courting death. I do not believe in coincidences, Sonnen."

"Nor do I," Sonnen growled. "Your mistake is thinking

that the attacker targeted Freyna. This is not the first time an assassin has been sent to kill Danil."

She frowned at him.

"The first attempt was made in Kailon," Danil voiced.

Tresa frowned. "To what end?"

"We have yet to discover who is behind it or why."

She set back, tapping her chin. "Let me see if I understand this. The human custodian was attacked on his own territory, but he was too weak to be aware of an imminent threat. He then brought the danger here, to the peril of our own custodian."

A flicker of orange flame showed in Sonnen's eyes. "Danil is hardly to blame."

"Oh, I'm aware." Tresa made a placating gesture. "He knows nothing of our ways, how our very kingdom rests upon the wellbeing of our leylines. He can hardly comprehend the risks he presents. The mistake, I fear, was in allowing him to become custodian in the first place."

Ice washed through Danil's bones. "The leylines chose me."

"As I understand it, few other options were available." Tresa regarded him coldly.

"That's not how leylines work," Danil seethed, although he internally feared that she was right.

"So you say."

"I suppose you have a remedy for it, then?" Sonnen questioned, his hand gripping the edge of the table.

"The High Council deals with many problems," Tresa said. She rose, smoothing down her robes. "Fear not, my prince. I won't send assassins to end your human's custodianship. But I will do what is best for Corros and Amas."

"And Kailon?" Danil asked.

Tresa gave him a dismissive look. "I have yet to see anything worth fighting for."

She bowed to Sonnen and swept out of the room.

Sonnen watched her leave, his expression brooding.

16

Late evening saw Hafryn return to their private quarters.

Danil sat in a chair close to the fire, his boots stretched out toward the warmth. He held the first crystal he'd brought with him from Kailon, turning it about in his hands. A calm sort of contentment emanated from the kiandrite, and when Danil pushed his senses into the precious stone, a trickle of power swept over him.

Noticing Danil, Hafryn paused in unclasping his cloak. "You've not slept."

Danil eyed him critically. "Nor have you."

The results of the cleansing ritual were starkly evident now. A bruise showed on Hafryn's cheek, others smattering darkly on his forearms. Shadows marred under his eyes, and there was a tightness about Hafryn's mouth that Danil hadn't seen before.

"I take it things aren't going so grandly for you, either," Danil said dryly.

Hafryn sank into the other chair with a groan. "We've made little headway if that's what you mean. But we at least know the assassin gained access to our rooms via the balcony."

"He flew up?" Danil frowned, setting aside the crystal. "Viren said the Eyrie aren't responsible this time."

"It serves him to believe so." Hafryn removed the tie holding back his red hair. It fell about his shoulders in loose waves. The wolf's eyes slid closed as he basked in the warmth.

Eyeing the cobwebs trapped on Hafryn's sleeve, Danil wondered where he'd been since the attack on Freyna. The wolf had always been secretive, but the events of the last few days left Danil feeling adrift.

Seeming to know his thoughts, Hafryn opened his eyes to study Danil. He face grew somber in the firelight. "I've fallen into old habits, *fala*," he admitted. "It won't happen again."

Danil raised an eyebrow. "You'll tell me about the Eyrie?"

Hafryn grimaced and straightened, hands clasped between his knees. "Have at it, then. What would you know, *fala*?"

"Viren."

Hafryn gave a wan smile. "We share a grandmother. I'm what you call a winter child—one born late in the mother's life. I was unexpected and too young to be of interest to my esteemed cousin, so I hardly knew him when he sent me packing." He shrugged. "It was nothing personal."

"Nothing personal," Danil murmured, again studying the bruises on the wolf's hands and face.

Hafryn waved the injuries aside. "Strength and cunning are the lifeblood of the Eyrie. The ritual was to ensure I hadn't softened during my time with the dragon prince."

"And Viren's satisfied?"

Hafryn shrugged and pointed to the pale blue mark on the inside of his elbow. "I still bear the House glyph."

"You know the cleansing was just an excuse to beat you."

The wolf hesitated. "Being an Eyrie is...complex. I didn't want to worry you."

Danil shook his head. "If it was really about strength and cunning, what you did in Kailon and Altonas should have been enough. You lured the magi into a trap and helped stop Magus Brianna from gaining control of Kailon."

Hafryn studied him in a new light. "You downplay your own role, Danil."

"Maybe, but we wouldn't have succeeded without you. If Tresa shared with the High Council what happened in Kailon, Viren would know that you risked your life to save Amas. So why test you at all?"

"I don't know. Petty grievances, perhaps. Either way, you have my word I won't fall into old traps. Or if I do, I'll be sure to have you at my back."

Danil snorted. "That's all I ask. *Fala*."

Hafryn paused, then covered his face and groaned. "I'd hoped you'd forgotten."

"Not likely." Danil couldn't suppress a grin. "If I'd known the meaning when you'd first said it—"

Hafryn pointed a finger at Danil. "You'd have gone running back to Roldaer, no matter that Magus Brianna wanted you dead."

"Possibly," Danil conceded, grin widening.

"*Possibly*," Hafryn muttered, his mouth twitching. "I meant it back then, Danil, but even more so now." He reached out and clasped Danil's hand. "I'm sorry I've given you reason to doubt me."

Sobering, Danil held tight. "No more secrets," he said.

"It's against my nature, but I'll do my best," Hafryn promised.

Danil nodded. "Good enough."

The lines about Hafryn's mouth eased. He cleared his throat. "Right. Well, I hear a great healer is being flown in to care for Freyna. She'll pull through."

"Can we see her?"

Hafryn hesitated. "Hopefully in the morning. We should let the healers do their work."

"Tresa blames me," Danil observed quietly.

"Common sense notwithstanding, eh? We knew she was dubious of your custodianship. At least now Tresa's showing her hand."

Danil gave Hafryn a narrow look, noticing he seemed largely unconcerned.

Hafryn winked. "You forget, *fala*, that everyone in Corros answers to Sonnen. Tresa holds less sway than she thinks." He tilted his head, listening. "Speaking of the prince—"

A low whump of dragon wings outside set the curtains to billowing. A few heartbeats later, Danil heard the thud of Sonnen's landing before the man stepped in from the balcony. He'd changed into plain breeches and embroidered nightshirt, his dark hair windswept. He pulled a makeshift knapsack out from under his cloak.

"Good. I'd hoped to see you both awake," Sonnen said, setting the knapsack upon the desk. He made a quelling motion when Danil and Hafryn made to stand and helped himself to a large dram from the carafe of spirits on the sideboard.

"And where have you been, oh dragon prince? Skulking about in the night isn't normally your style," Hafryn narrowed his eyes as he took in the way Sonnen hovered around the knapsack. "Or thievery, for that matter."

Sonnen picked up the knapsack and grabbed an ornately embroidered footstool to sit with his back to the fire. "You are not the only one in search of information, wolf."

"Thievery," Hafryn pressed. "You're among friends, Sonnen. We won't besmirch your honor."

Sonnen bared his teeth in a humorless smile. "I prefer the term borrowing—especially when it involves searching Freyna's quarters."

"Really." Hafryn leaned forward, his eyebrows raised. "Freyna is above reproach, Sonnen."

Danil eyed the knapsack, unable to hold back his growing curiosity. "It's about that word she said, isn't it? *Videre.*" He remembered the desperation in her eyes when she'd spoken.

The dragon gave a pleased rumble. "You are quick to understand the heart of matters, custodian."

It had seemed more critical to Freyna than saving her own energy.

"Can't say I know the word," Hafryn said with a frown.

"Nor I," Sonnen replied and scrunched his face in thought. "It has a ring of Old Amasian though. There may be something useful in Freyna's notes and readings—I took what I believe are the most likely tomes."

The knapsack was crammed to the brim with various sized books.

"Great. I remember the last time we dealt with an old tome," Hafryn muttered and unconsciously rubbed his hands on his breeches.

"Hmm, yes. We were able to thwart a magi plot," Sonnen pointed out. He turned to Danil. "I can only assume something happened during your time with Freyna this morning, Danil, that made the term important to Freyna."

Danil rubbed the back of his neck. "It looks like that I can see hidden glyphs—or at least the protective glyphs within the catacombs."

Sonnen frowned. "Those glyphs ensure the safety of our magical knowledge, Danil. Not even our greatest enchanters know their exact position or design."

He gave a helpless shrug. "I didn't mean to. It just happened."

The dragon prince studied him, his expression meditative. "You continue to confound me, Danil."

"It's what makes people so nervous," Hafryn pointed out.

Sonnen waved the comment aside. "Until Freyna can explain herself, we must discover all that we can. *Videre* is unmistakably Amasian, and so the knowledge lies here somewhere."

Hafryn pushed himself out of his chair. He took the knapsack and upended it onto the floor. "Right, then. Grab a book, Danil. We're in for a long night."

17

Morning saw Danil yawning blearily into the pages. The pilfered books and tomes lay spread about the sitting room's main table, with Hafryn slouched in the chair opposite him as he read. Servants entered to place plates of steaming bread and fruit amidst the mess, and Danil stretched stiffly. Having learned enough about the properties of fungi for treating rashes and warts to last a lifetime, he slapped the book closed and reached for the thinnest, smallest tome lying amongst the mess.

Hafryn watched over the top of his book and snorted.

Danil's eyes narrowed. "What?"

"I believe that's a treatise on Eliar undergarments," Hafryn said, eyes twinkling. "It was quite the fad here a few summers past."

Danil groaned. "Why did Sonnen take it from Freyna's rooms, then?"

"I daresay our illustrious leader panicked," Hafryn said with a grin. "Skulking about isn't his usual style."

He couldn't help but smile at that. The thought of

Sonnen tiptoeing about Freyna's rooms seemed ridiculous. "Have you found anything?" Danil asked eventually.

"Freyna's interests are certainly varied," Hafryn said, flipping a page. "But I've had no luck here."

"Seems to be the way of things lately," Danil muttered, slumping. He grabbed a small bun dotted with nuts and slathered it with butter before handing half to Hafryn.

The wolf murmured his thanks. "We may just have to wait until Freyna is well enough to explain herself." He closed his book with a sigh. "In the meantime, you have to prepare for the High Council."

Danil paled. "I thought with Freyna injured—"

Hafryn shook his head. "An assassin in our midst makes everyone nervous. The High Council will want to hear from you as soon as possible, if only to get you out of Corros sooner."

"Great," Danil muttered.

Sonnen entered the sitting room dressed in a simple tunic and breeches. His feet were bare on the cold granite. "Hafryn indeed has the right of it, Danil," he murmured as he took a seat. "But it is to our advantage. We need the council to move quickly."

"And the threat of danger dangling overhead might be just what we need to get them to finally agree on something," Hafryn agreed.

Sonnen spooned honey over a roll. "No shifter is beyond personal need, Danil. Not even the High Council."

It only made the ball in his belly grow heavier. "How can I get them to listen when they doubt my legitimacy?"

"Only to those who have not met you cast doubt," Sonnen replied. "You will sway them."

Danil had no idea what the dragon expected him to do.

"I'll go with him," Hafryn muttered.

Sonnen shook his head. "There are times when a custodian must stand alone." His golden eyes settled on Danil. "You have already proven yourself capable. I believe you will serve Kailon well once again."

Taking a deep breath, Danil nodded.

A knock on the door broke the moment.

A guard stepped inside and bowed. "Councilor Viren wishes to speak with you, my prince."

Sonnen sat back, wiping his hands on a napkin. "This ought to be good. Show him in."

The Eyrie councilor strode inside and gave the room a sweeping bow. "Apologies for my interruption," he said.

Sonnen waved to an empty seat. "Join us, honored councilor."

"Thank you, Prince Sonnen, but I'll keep this short." Viren turned to Danil, who felt his innards tighten under the sharp regard. "The attack in the deadlands was carried out by an assassin of the High Reaches. A woman most skilled in her craft. Her first failure appears to have been her last." He pulled a roll of parchment from his pouch. "This is her contract."

Hafryn got up and walked the contract to Sonnen. They both quickly scanned the paper. "This doesn't reveal the identity of the person who bought her contract."

"It's how we have always conducted our business," Viren said. "But my people have...ways of finding out." Viren's eyes slid back to Danil. He bowed. "What happened in Kailon was an aberration, done without the permission of a Keeper. The Eyrie do not kill custodians."

"You ignore all evidence to the contrary, Viren." Sonnen thumbed the parchment. "Nonetheless, your assassin must have been offered a hefty price to go against the will of her House."

"She wouldn't have lived long to enjoy the spoils of her contract," Viren said. "Such killings have consequences for all involved. Whoever bought the contract was wise not to come to me first."

Hafryn folded his arms. "You're a Keeper. You expect us to believe you had no idea what your assassins were up to?"

Viren appeared unperturbed. "I arrived in Corros only a day before you—after, I believe, the attack in the deadlands."

"Convenient." Hafryn squinted at the man.

"Apparently so, cousin," Viren replied, mouth tilting upwards. "I assure you I have not signed off on any new contracts since."

Danil resisted the urge to shiver.

"Had the attack in the deadlands succeeded, the responsibility would have fallen on you, Viren," Sonnen rumbled, his warning clear.

The Eyrie councilor inclined his head. "Yes, my prince. It's why I wish to offer the services of the Eyrie to protect the custodian."

Silence filled the sitting room.

"Beg pardon?" Sonnen said.

"A detail of my personal guards." Viren bowed respectfully. "For the deadlands custodian."

Danil's mouth fell open. The Eyrie councilor kept his expression bland.

Sonnen sat back, his expression contemplative.

"You can't be serious, Sonnen!" Hafryn blurted out. "We already know the Eyrie are responsible."

"For the first attempt," Sonnen said contemplatively. "The attack on Freyna was clumsily done. Such incompetence suggests the folk who seek Danil's death have made alternative arrangements."

Viren inclined his head. "That is our belief, also, my prince. Nonetheless, the Eyrie must make reparations for what happened in the deadlands." His gaze slid back to Danil. "Although I am curious to know how you survived, custodian. She was one of our finest assets."

Danil's skin pebbled under the cool regard. "Luck," he muttered, resisting the urge to fold his arms.

The Eyrie councilor smiled. "It appears you have that in abundance."

Danil held Viren's gaze, watching as amusement settled in his green eyes. They reminded him suddenly of Hafryn at his most mischievous, and he had to look away.

"Are we agreed, my prince?" Viren asked. "The custodian's luck cannot run true forever."

"Very well," Sonnen said after a considered pause.

Scowling, Danil bit back the urge to argue, and instead hoped Sonnen knew what he was doing. Hafryn seemed doubtful, muttering under his breath.

"You will select these guards yourself, Councilor Viren," Sonnen continued. "Their conduct will reflect on you." Flames showed in his eyes.

Viren bowed. "Of course, my prince. I will get onto it immediately." He bowed again before striding for the door. It closed behind him with a soft snick.

Hafryn folded his arms. "Ten gold crowns the guards are already in the corridor," he muttered. He turned to Sonnen. "This is madness. We can't trust the Eyrie."

Sonnen grunted. "We can expect them to hold to their honor, Hafryn. Viren is many things, but he stays true to his word. I believe having Eyrie guards will be to our benefit."

"Aye, until it isn't," Hafryn muttered.

Sonnen inclined his head. "Perhaps so."

A knock interrupted any further conversation.

Hafryn threw up his hands. "What now?" he muttered.

An aging woman in brown robes bowed deeply.

Sonnen rose to his feet. "Honored healer," he said as he returned the bow.

"Custodian Freyna has awakened, my prince," the woman said. "She would speak with you now."

Danil pulled back his chair.

Sonnen raised a hand. "You must prepare for the High Council, Danil. They are expecting you shortly."

Danil gaped. "But—"

"I will give the custodian your regards." The dragon's expression was implacable.

Feeling his face heat, Danil sank back in his chair. "I'd appreciate it."

Hafryn frowned. "I'd go with you to see if Freyna's up for some questions, Sonnen, but I'll feel better joining Danil's escort."

Sonnen nodded as he joined the healer. "That might be for the best."

18

As Hafryn suspected, four Eyrie guards stood at attention outside. Red haired and green-eyed, their kinship with Hafryn was obvious. One eyed at Hafryn with her lip curled but otherwise did nothing. The remaining three kept their gazed fixedly straight ahead as if Hafryn didn't exist.

Hafryn resolutely ignored them, strolling beside Danil with an air of nonchalance. The Eyrie fell in behind them.

Squinting, Danil willed himself to see their Trueforms. Four russet wolves trotted the corridor, pausing at various doors and archways as if checking for danger. Danil's eyebrow quirked in surprise as Hafryn's Trueform loped ahead to scrutinize any approaching shifter.

"What is it?" Hafryn asked as they took a set of stairs to the upper levels.

Danil shook his head. Hafryn's wolf tilted its head, tongue lolling as it trotted back toward him. It gave his hand a gentle lick, and Danil smiled gratefully. "I'm just glad you're here."

Hafryn winked.

They neared the double doors leading into the High Council chambers. Two guards stood at the entrance, and opposite them was Arlyn's two attendants. Seeing their approach, one guard rapped on the door.

A chamberlain in officious robes emerged, sweaty and apprehensive.

"Custodian Danil," he said and gave a hasty bow. "The High Council does not require you this day."

Danil blinked.

Hafryn pushed in front. "Say again?"

"The High Council is attending to other matters," the chamberlain said and licked his lip nervously. "They will call for you when needed."

"Well, we need to speak with them now," Hafryn growled. "The custodian has been here for days. You might not be aware, but there's a certain urgency to matters requiring the High Council's approval."

"It will not be this day."

The two Roldaerian attendants ignored them, faces carefully blank.

"Emissary Arlyn is speaking with the High Council again," Danil guessed as he eyed the red robed soldiers.

Hafryn's growl deepened. "So the High Council speaks with a foreign ambassador twice before seeing a custodian."

The chamberlain frowned. "The custodian is also foreign, no?"

Hafryn's mouth opened to argue.

"The High Council is very firm," the chamberlain interrupted, chest puffing as he stood between the two guards. "They will not hear the Roldaerian custodian today." He bowed and stepped back into the chamber, the door firmly shutting after him.

Danil gaped. "*Roldaerian* custodian?"

Cursing, Hafryn said, "Let's find Sonnen."

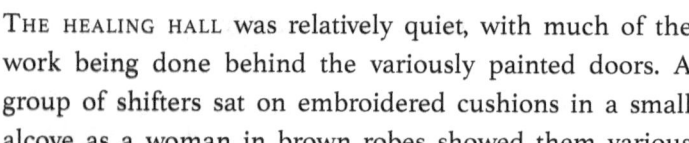

THE HEALING HALL was relatively quiet, with much of the work being done behind the variously painted doors. A group of shifters sat on embroidered cushions in a small alcove as a woman in brown robes showed them various leaves and plants.

Movement caught his eye as a yellow door opened. A ghostlike snow leopard emerged to pad across the hall toward them. To Danil's surprise, she butted her head against his hand. Lines of iridescent light showed along her spine and the tips of her claws. It reminded him suddenly of Freyna's lightning-filled Trueform.

"Danil," Elania called as she stepped out of the healing room. She wore a thick wayfarer's cloak over tunic and breeches dyed dappled green to match the changing forest landscape of Kailon. Her hair appeared wind tousled about her face.

"When did you get here?" Danil asked in delight as she clasped his arm.

"Griff flew me in. He volunteered, apparently," Elania said, her voice rich with bemusement. She gripped Hafryn's forearm. "It's good to see you both well."

Hafryn nodded. "And you. How goes it with Freyna?"

Elania winked. "Our beloved custodian is not done with this world yet. She'll recover in time."

The tension in Danil's shoulders eased. "You're the great healer they sent for," he realized.

Her cheeks dimpled. "That's high praise indeed, Danil. Thank you."

"It's well earned," Hafryn said, smiling.

"But why aren't you permanently in Corros?" Danil asked Elania. Someone with her skills would be in constant demand in a citadel this large.

"Sonnen doesn't send riffraff and scoundrels to the borderland, *fala*," Hafryn said with a grin.

"Speak for yourself," Elania laughed. "Though it's true that our dragon prince might have needed a moment's convincing. I had my reasons to insist."

"I assume one of those reasons remains in Kailon," Hafryn said with a cheeky grin. "How fares Blutark, in any case?"

A faint pink filled Elania's cheeks. "Just fine, Hafryn," she said tartly. "I'll be sure to give him your regards when I head back." She returned to Danil. "Kailon is a fitting name for the deadlands. Its forests grow richer every day."

The tension in his belly eased. "I can feel it, though it's good to hear you say it," Danil said.

A sudden yearning took him. He missed the gentle buzz of energy beneath his feet at Kailon and the simple enjoyment of watching trees grow. The crystal seemed to grow heavier around his neck.

Hafryn clapped a hand on his shoulder. "We'll turn the High Council to our cause."

Danil could only hope he was right.

Elania continued to study the guards. "What's with the Eyrie?"

They stood a respectful distance away, their expressions bland.

"A bit of posturing," Hafryn muttered, eyes darkening. "Viren isn't a supporter of Danil, but he enjoys keeping people off balance." He shook himself. "Sonnen still inside? Has Freyna spoken of who attacked her?"

Elania shook her head. "Her recollections are vague,

unfortunately." She paused. "There was mention of a panther."

"Panther?" Danil blurted, startled. "I thought the assassin came in through the balcony."

Hafryn's face turned grim. "Someone must have aided him—I know of no panthers who can scale cliffs in such a manner."

That certainly complicated matters. Danil swallowed his dismay.

"What else?" Hafryn pressed Elania. "There's little left of our would-be assassin to go on."

"She's very weak, Hafryn," Elania explained. "It's surprising that she held out long enough for me to come, though I suppose it helped that Griff hardly stopped to rest on our journey."

"It wouldn't be the first time a custodian has cheated death," Hafryn muttered. He sighed. "Very well. It's more than we had to go on earlier today, at least."

"Did Freyna mention anything else?" Danil asked. "Like what happened in the catacombs?"

She shook her head. "I'm afraid not, Danil."

The rustle of cloth made Danil turn to see a young man in healer robes.

"Custodian Freyna would speak with you, Custodian Danil," he said with a respectful bow.

Danil threw Hafryn a startled look.

Elania shrugged. "Sonnen is with her still, trying to piece events together."

The young man motioned Danil to follow.

Danil trailed after him to a private room. It was plainly adorned with a bed and side table with a basin of water. A chair sat beside the bed, a small window above it showing swiftly moving clouds and the peak of a nearby mountain.

Sonnen leaned against the wall, a slight breeze pulling his dark hair.

Freyna seemed to be asleep, her white hair spread about her on the pillow and blankets pulled up to her chin. She appeared frail in a way Danil hadn't considered possible.

"Don't stay overlong," the young healer spoke softly before closing the door with a gentle click.

Sonnen pointed to the chair.

Lowering himself, Danil delicately took Freyna's hand.

Her eyes opened a crack. Seeing him, she smiled slightly. "Honored custodian," she murmured.

His eyes suddenly stung. "Honored custodian," he repeated with a bow of his head.

"Shh, not your fault," Freyna rasped.

Danil nodded, struggling to free the words lodged in his throat.

"You've been searching my books," she murmured, mouth tilting slightly as she looked to Sonnen.

"Yes, Hafryn and I. That word—"

"*Videre.*" She weakly tapped the corner of her eye.

Danil said, "No one seems to know it."

"The ability to See," she murmured, eyes closing. "I could teach you—" She coughed suddenly.

Danil grabbed the cup of water on the side table, helping her sit up to drink.

Taking fragile sips, Freyna collapsed back with a sigh. "Another time, Danil. But know that custodians are unique among Amas. Our enchantments are not our own."

Danil tried his best to understand. "You mean the leylines decide."

She nodded, her eyes sliding shut again.

Danil sat back in the chair. "The first time I saw a Trueform—" He stopped, swallowing.

"It was a time of great need," Sonnen murmured, his voice a deep rumble in the small room.

"Yes," Danil whispered.

Freyna gave an echo of a smile. "Concentrate, and you will see far more."

"But I don't know what I'm doing," he admitted in frustration.

She patted his hand gently. "Few of us ever really do."

It was hardly helpful. Even now, Emissary Arlyn was swaying the High Council to her demands. Danil could not entertain the thought that the results would be good for Kailon.

He couldn't shake the sense of approaching danger. With the High Council refusing to even see him, he feared time was running out.

"You should revisit the first crystal, Danil," Freyna murmured. "I can feel it calling for you."

Startled, Danil leaned forward. "Does it know what *videre* means—can it show me?"

She squeezed his hand. "Be careful. It doesn't always give you the answers you want."

"I will. Thank you, Freyna." He studied her pale face. She seemed smaller somehow. The edge of a bandage showed at her collarbone. "Will you be okay?"

Freyna's eyes opened, the irises mellow. "I am not done with this world yet," she murmured. "Although it is indeed nearing the time that I announce my search for a successor."

Sonnen huffed. "A bit premature, Freyna."

She waved a hand. "You simply can't abide the posturing of those who think themselves deserving," she replied. "You prefer folk who don't yet know the measure of their potential."

The dragon prince folded his arms.

Danil thought of Elania and the veins of light running through her Trueform. They were so like Freyna's own iridescent bird, which sat at the end of the bed looking ragged but stubborn.

Freyna's gaze momentarily sharpened. "You see much for someone new to our ways, Danil."

He shook his head. "I hope to one day have your insight."

She smiled and settled back into the pillows. "One challenge at a time, custodian."

19

Danil left the healing hall and found Hafryn waiting for him on a bench seat in the corridor outside. The wolf shifter leaped to his feet, face brimming with questions.

"Care to join me in the catacombs?" Danil asked.

"Of course," Hafryn said with a raised eyebrow and fell into step beside him. "But first, how's Freyna?"

"She says she'll be fine." It eased a knot in his belly.

The four Eyrie guards peeled away from their station at the end of the corridor, following at a respectful distance.

"Custodians are known for their stubbornness." Hafryn bumped his shoulder affectionately against Danil's. "Elania is headed off on some errands now that the greatest danger has passed. She says to stay out of trouble until she can join in."

Danil couldn't help but smile. "I hope you didn't make any promises."

Hafryn gave a soft huff. "Hardly. Did you tell Sonnen about the High Council?"

Shaking his head, Danil said, "It didn't seem the place, not with Freyna so weakened."

"At least we have a lead on her attacker."

Danil eyed Hafryn as they strode down a stairwell. The air felt cooler as they neared the arched entrance to the catacombs, though there was no dampness like the tunnels he was used to in Kailon.

"I don't suppose Elania's errands have anything to do with finding the panther?" Danil asked.

A chagrined gleam showed in Hafryn's eyes.

Danil paused under the catacomb archway. "You can't ask me to sit around again, Hafryn. I won't do it."

The wolf shifter faltered, clearly wanting to argue. He sighed. "If Elania finds something of interest, we'll deal with it together."

"Finally," Danil grunted and took the water-smooth corridor leading to the first crystal.

Shouts rang out behind them, and Danil flinched instinctively. The Eyrie retreated from the entrance, pointing at the glyphs on the archway. The glyphs shone gold with flashes of red. One Eyrie attempted to approach again, but an invisible force seemed to hold her still.

"Are you doing that?" Hafryn asked, gaping.

Shaking his head, Danil said, "I wouldn't know how."

Hafryn suddenly grinned in realization. He swaggered back toward the entrance, eyeing the archway. "Looks like you folk aren't welcome in the catacombs," he told the Eyrie with a wink.

The woman bared her teeth.

With a jaunty wave, Hafryn said, "By all means, wait for our return." He ambled back to Danil.

Danil waited until they were out of earshot. "I'm not sure they appreciate your humor, Hafryn."

The wolf huffed. "The cleansing ritual means they can't use violence for another ten days. Besides, I'm more of an irritant than an enemy of consequence."

Danil hoped they'd long returned to Kailon before the Eyrie decided otherwise.

They entered the chamber. The first crystal flamed gold and red to match the archway outside but suddenly turned blue as if noticing Danil's arrival. The smaller stone about his neck trilled in his mind.

Hafryn loitered at the doorway. "What exactly did Freyna want you to do here?"

Shrugging, Danil said, "She wasn't specific. Just that I should be here." He circled the huge crystal. Little bursts of light pulsed from its depths.

Arms folded, Hafryn muttered something under his breath. Danil thought he heard the words 'custodian' and 'mysticism'. He snorted.

"Freyna wouldn't waste our time," Danil said.

"Aye, but she's not exactly at her best right now," Hafryn muttered.

Lifting his gaze to the highest point of the crystal, Danil said, "I think she suggested coming here for that very reason. She said *videre* are people who See."

"See what, *fala*?"

He shrugged helplessly.

Part of the crystal darkened to deep azure and formed the shape of a hand in its depths. It seemed to pull at Danil. His fingers twitched in response.

Hafryn pushed off the doorway. "This doesn't seem wise." He drew close. "There are stories of first crystals causing death and mauling of folk who dared touch them."

The hand-shaped light pulsed steadily.

"I hope this is an invitation, then," Danil murmured.

Against his better judgment, he touched the crystal.

The roar of flames filled his ears, his sight smothered by a red veil. Smoke bit deep into his lungs. Danil's throat constricted.

The red veil lifted. Two figures strode through the banked fire. One was a man, broad-shouldered and brooding. Behind him was a grotesquely misshapen Trueform, blackened with a horse's body but a strange, melted head discernible only by cold blue eyes and exposed teeth.

"Kaul," Danil breathed, trembling.

His companion, a white-haired woman with a cloak pulled tight about her, knelt atop a slab of granite. Behind her was the tunnel leading down to the Temple of Kaul. At her feet was a glyph. Danil recognized the strange silvery glow. It matched the protective glyphs hidden from sight in the catacombs.

The hairs on the back of Danil's neck rose.

She chiseled the pattern of the glyph into the stone, then diffidently moved aside.

With sharpened claws studded with reddened kiandrite, Kaul raked across the glyph. The light sputtered. Kaul wove a symbol in the air, watching as it took shape and then sank into the ground.

The glyph died.

Danil felt the wrenching pain of it in his chest.

The woman suddenly spied Danil through the smoke. "*Videre,*" she growled. Pulling a blade from her belt, she stormed toward him.

Danil backed up, arms out. His boot caught on a ledge of stone, and he fell backward.

"Danil!"

He came to himself on his back a few feet away from the

crystal. Sweat filmed his face. His lungs hardly seemed to work.

Hafryn gripped his shoulders, shaking them, his green eyes panicked. "*Danil!*"

"I'm—" He coughed, then sucked in cool air. "I'm okay. I'm here."

"You disappeared!" Hafryn's voice rang out in the chamber. "There was no trace of you!"

Hands trembling, Danil wiped his face. "I went— somewhere? There was Kaul. He did something to a glyph, killed it. He destroyed the glyph on purpose."

Hafryn sat back on his heels, pale-faced and shaken.

Easing himself up to sitting, Danil gazed up at the crystal. It glowed a mellow, satisfied blue. "Kaul had a companion. She was helping him find hidden glyphs. I—I think she was *videre*." His gaze fell back to Hafryn. "She knew I was the same. How could she know that, Hafryn? How did she even notice me?"

"I don't know, but let's get out of here." The wolf helped Danil up onto his feet.

Momentarily dizzy, Danil thought he saw the ruined glyph take shape within the light of the crystal. He blinked, and it was gone.

"I'd prefer if we didn't linger, *fala.* Losing you once is enough for today." Hafryn's voice was shaky as he threw one of Danil's arms across his shoulder and half-carried him out of the chamber.

"We have to tell the High Council," Danil stated.

"Tell them what? That you had a vision that showed a woman helping Kaul strip us of our enchanter heritage?" Hafryn growled. "And that you share her exact same talents?"

Danil bit his lip in understanding.

Hafryn eased him onto a bench seat. He threw an anxious look toward the arched entrance to the catacombs. "Catch your breath. But say nothing until we can speak of this to Sonnen."

Danil nodded, defeated. The taste of smoke lingered in his mouth.

20

V iren waited for them outside the catacombs.

Somewhat steadier on his feet, Danil nonetheless felt a moment of disorientation as the Eyrie councilor's Trueform paced the length of floor just beyond the archway. Its russet coat bristled in agitation. Viren himself appeared calm, green eyes mild. He leaned against the stone wall beside the stairs, arms folded in such a familiar manner that Danil couldn't help but think of Hafryn.

Hafryn muttered something under his breath. They strode under the archway without so much as a spark of light from the glyphs.

"Are you done being a fool, Hafryn?" Viren asked as he straightened. The four guards waited at the base of the stairs, expressions sour.

Hafryn released a humorless laugh. "Pretty sure I'm not, but for reasons different to whatever you're referring to, cousin."

Viren fell in step with them as they climbed the stairs. "The assassin, *cousin*. Your enemies may yet send another, but you let the human walk about unprotected."

"The catacombs are hardly unprotected," Danil muttered.

The Eyrie councilor gave him a hard, assessing look.

"You sound like you've found something," Hafryn said, his eyes narrow.

"Sonnen discussed what Custodian Freyna saw of her attacker," Viren hedged.

Hafryn slowed. "And?" he pressed.

Viren smiled. "Panthers are by nature rather solitary, so they tend to get noticed. One such fellow happened to rent accommodation down at the harbor square—paid up for a week and hasn't been seen for a few days. Not since your human's would-be assassin met his end, in any case."

Straightening, Danil said to Hafryn, "Sounds like a decent lead."

Viren nodded. "The innkeeper is of a mind to throw out the panther's possessions. There might be something useful to prove he was indeed your would-be assassin."

"And perhaps information about whoever paid for his services." Hafryn eyed Danil. "Care for a bit of snooping?"

Startled, Danil asked, "What about Sonnen?"

"I understand Sonnen is in meetings with Councilor Tresa," Viren said. He paused in thought. "It may be fine to wait until after you've attended to whatever is so pressing with the prince."

Hafryn scrubbed his chin. "We may lose our chance if the innkeeper throws out that gear before we have our chance."

Viren gave a smooth smile. "I can send a few of my people in your stead, cousin."

"A generous offer," Hafryn said, baring teeth in his own humorless grin. "I'd prefer to see for myself."

The Eyrie councilor bowed his head.

Danil bit his lip. "I'm not staying behind," he muttered. With a nod, he added, "And in truth, if it means getting out of Corros for a span, lead on."

They took one of the outer stairwells that followed the juts and plateaus of the cliffs. Unlit lamps dotted the path.

Danil felt drawn to the vista of the harbor town below. It stretched out along the banks of the lake. A few skiffs rode the serene water. Three piers jutted far into the depths, and Danil could make out sailors and tradesfolk with their wares displayed on the wooden boardwalks.

The path widened to allow wagons into the lower levels of the citadel. Danil stepped to the side to enable a caravaner to clatter past, her wares clanging beneath the canvas.

The road followed the gentle curve of the lake, the buildings a mixture of single and two-story structures with inner courtyards lined with plants and brightly colored urns and bench chairs. Larges pockets of trees and fernery took up sections of the township, all surrounded by cobbled streets and buildings. Danil had never seen the like. Overhead, Corros was a glittering mass of balconies and stairwells, with flashes of kiandrite painting the cliff in golds and blues.

The inn stood close to the central pier. It was a simple, two-story building with a thatched roof and stone steps leading into the aleroom. A warm glow filtered through the shutters, and within came the sound of laughter and the strum of a lute.

A sudden wash of homesickness swept over Danil.

The inn reminded him of Farin. He rarely thought of his home village, nor the people he'd lost so that King Liam could launch his war against Amas. He felt far removed from the deadland scavenger who'd once dared to steal a magi book.

Hafryn slowed to match his pace. "What is it?"

Shaking his thoughts loose, Danil murmured, "Nothing."

Hafryn watched him a moment longer before nodding. "Let's get upstairs."

The four guards stayed outside as they entered the aleroom filled with late afternoon patrons. A bard sat on a chair in one corner, strumming a ditty and tightening the strings of her lute.

Viren handed the serving woman a gold coin, bending close to murmur in her ear.

She indicated the stairs behind the bar.

Upstairs in a dimly-lit corridor, Viren strode to the very end. The Eyrie councilor eased the door open to the darkened room and quietly slipped inside.

Hafryn paused to draw his dagger. "Stay cautious, *fala*."

Danil nodded.

The room was finer than Danil expected, with an ornately carved bed and large dresser. A woven rug covered much of the floor. At the foot of the bed was a battered traveling trunk that seemed incongruous with the rest of the room.

Hafryn made for the trunk, rifling through the contents of tunics and undergarments. "Check the dresser," he said to Danil with a point of his chin.

Pulling open the drawers, Danil shook his head in dismay. "Empty." He tapped the edges of the drawers, hoping for a hidden compartment. Old Minna from Farin had liked to hide her fire-ale from her daughters by stashing it in the back of her dresser.

Viren kicked back the rug, walking the floorboards with

slow, measured steps. His Trueform sat in the doorway, head tilted as if listening intently for false boards and other smuggler tricks.

Hafryn sat back on his heels, scowling. "There's little of interest here. Certainly nothing to connect the missing panther to our assassin."

"Do you think someone's been here before us?" Danil asked as he closed the dresser.

"This was a stretch even by Eyrie standards." Hafryn rapped his fingers on the top of the trunk. "Viren?"

The man nudged the rug back into place. "I didn't send anyone ahead to pull your tail, cousin. My people had little to go on before the custodian awoke."

Muttering under his breath, Hafryn lifted the feather-stuffed pallet. "Aha!" He pulled out a small trinket box no larger than his palm. "Not the place I'd put it, but our assassin doesn't seem to be particularly smart."

Peering over his shoulder, Danil saw the box was made of plain wood, with only two glyphs etched near the hinge. Hafryn ran his thumb over the latch, and one of the glyphs glowed a sullen red. Hafryn seemed not to notice.

"Wait," Danil said. He took the box from Hafryn and turned it about. He gently nudged the latch, nodding when the glyph darkened to congealed blood. "See?"

Hafryn gave him a blank look. "I'm afraid I don't, *fala*."

"The—oh," Danil paused, frowning. "How many glyphs do you count?"

Stepping close, Viren said, "This one here is a maker's mark—the box came from the lakelands district within Eyrie, though you shouldn't take it as an admission of guilt."

Danil resisted a snort.

"There are no other markings that I can see," Viren

finished. His hand skipped over the red glyph as if averse to touching it.

The glyph set Danil's nerves on edge. "I don't think we should open the box."

Viren gave an annoyed huff.

Hafryn, however, took Danil at his word. "Let's get an enchanter to check it over, just to be safe." He tucked the box under his tunic. "Chin up, *fala*. It looks like we finally found something."

THEY RETURNED to Corros as magelights filtered soft light through the night-filled archways.

Viren bid them farewell in the lower levels. His Trueform loped to a nearby stairwell, tail jaunty like a streamer. The four Eyrie guards remained with Danil and Hafryn.

Bone weary, Danil trudged up to a balcony filled with night revelers. The spiced aromas of a large banquet sat heavy in the air. Long tables lined the dining hall within.

Hafryn frowned as he peered amongst the throng.

"Danil!"

Arlyn pulled herself away from the balcony party. Her officious robes were heavy with silver embroidery. The crest of Roldaer glinted in the magelight.

"Wonderful news, is it not?" She beamed.

Danil mustered a bow. "I'm not sure what you speak of, emissary."

Arlyn hooked her arm through his. "The High Council's decision, of course! There were a few concessions on both sides, naturally, but the deadlands shall return to neutral territory once again."

Ears suddenly ringing, Danil blurted, "What?"

Hafryn pushed his way between them. "We've been outside the citadel, emissary, and weren't here for the announcement."

Arlyn affected a look of confusion. "The High Council reached an agreement this morning. It's been all anyone can talk about today."

With a flash of understanding, Danil realized Viren had taken part in the decision before joining them at the harbor inn. "Why didn't Viren say anything?"

Hafryn's teeth clenched. "Why indeed," he gritted out.

Arlyn smiled again, though her eyes were sharp. "Well, your aid will be most welcome, Danil. You, too, Hafryn. Although there can be no more Amasian camps in the deadlands, I'm afraid. But it's scarcely a place one visits willingly anyway." She laughed gaily.

A wave of despair seized Danil. There was no way he could protect Kailon. Not on his own. "But I haven't spoken to the High Council yet."

Hafryn suddenly gripped Danil's arm. "Excuse us, emissary." He steered Danil off the balcony, away from Arlyn's knowing gaze.

Numb, Danil let himself be guided into a quiet corridor, far from the noise and bustle of the celebrations. "Hafryn," he said dazedly. "The magi can't be allowed near Kailon. They won't treat it like neutral territory."

Tightening his grip, Hafryn said, "Perhaps Arlyn exaggerates."

"They're rejoicing in there, Hafryn. Like war has been averted." Shoulders slumping, Danil added, "I saw the council members."

"I know," Hafryn muttered. He directed Danil up a set of stairs. "I never imagined they'd bargain away kiandrite and leylines for a mere whiff of safety. Roldaer has threatened us with war for decades, but we've always dismissed their demands."

Danil slowed as a new realization dawned. "Arlyn saw us dig out the first crystal—she'll tell the magi."

"If her soldiers back at Farin haven't already," Hafryn agreed. He trotted up the stairwell. "Come on, *fala*. We need Sonnen—or Griff, really. Time to leave this place and return to where we belong."

Realizing Hafryn meant to journey back to Kailon, Danil said, "But the treaty. If what Arlyn says is true, there can't be any Amasians in Kailon."

Hafryn spun about, suddenly angry. "Kailon belongs to neither Amas or Roldaer. Are you going to let those arrogant rats back there dictate its fate?"

That steeled Danil. "No," he swore. If Amas would not lend aid, then they'd stop Roldaer themselves. Even if he had little idea how. "It won't be easy, Hafryn. Are you sure you want to go back? This is your chance to be free of this mess."

Hafryn trod down the steps so that they were at a level. He cupped Danil's face, green eyes earnest. "Being with you has guided my steps for longer than you know, *fala*."

It set a low heat in Danil's belly. He pressed his mouth to Hafryn's, hoping it would convey how deeply he felt. "Thank you," he whispered.

Hafryn pulled back, smirking. "Besides, who wouldn't want to be the dashing lover of a custodian?" He strode up the stairs with a swagger.

"Dashing?" Danil raised an eyebrow as he trotted to catch up.

"I've been restraining myself, *fala*," he admitted. He

raised a finger. "But no more. If we're to battle Roldaer, they'll get the full measure of me."

"Sounds frightening."

Hafryn huffed a laugh.

A shadow crossed above them at the top of the stairs. In the uncertain light, a handful of shifters emerged to crowd the steps. Danil thought he saw the flash of a drawn blade. Then a ghostly, blue-winged owl glided down toward them.

"Hafryn," Danil hissed.

But it was too late. As many as a dozen red-haired Eyrie strangers blocked the stairs below them, also. To Danil's alarm, their four guards drew their swords and joined the Eyrie ranks.

Cursing, Hafryn ushered Danil close to the wall before he pulled out his blade.

"Don't make a fuss," a plain-faced woman ordered. She strode down the stairs, her pace leisurely as she wove a symbol into the air.

Danil wondered if these were assassins sent by his mysterious enemy. He felt the moment the enchantment swept over them. Voices and the scuff of footsteps beyond the stairwell grew suddenly silent, and Danil realized whatever happened here, he and Hafryn were alone in facing it.

"Stay close," Hafryn muttered as they moved back to back. "There's not enough space for them to all come at once."

Dagger in a sweaty grip, Danil waited with dull dread. The Eyrie made no pretense as to their intentions. They strode the stairs to form a menacing half circle around Danil and Hafryn.

"What about the ritual?" Danil asked desperately. It was supposed to protect Hafryn from harm by his own people.

Hafryn snorted. "You think these traitors are following Viren's orders?"

The plain-faced woman smirked. "It's fortunate you care for him, custodian."

Danil was entirely sure she meant otherwise.

A heartbeat later, the Eyrie attacked. Shouts rang off the walls as Hafryn cut his first assailant across the thigh before stabbing another in the chest. The Eyrie facing Danil were more hesitant, perhaps leery of the consequences of attacking a custodian. Danil pressed the advantage, lashing out in a panicked frenzy.

Then his vision flickered to reveal a massive wolf watching placidly from the top of the stairs.

Viren, he realized in horror.

An Eyrie brought up her shield to slam it in Danil's face. It rocked him off his feet. He sensed Hafryn scrambling to protect him, shouting, but then a boot slammed down. More rapidly followed.

Blackness stole him away.

21

Danil groggily woke to the sound of rushing water.

Face feeling like a single throbbing bruise, he staggered to his feet to find himself in the cargo hold of a small ship. Sunlight streamed in through a grate overhead, while the low murmur of voices and the pad of bare feet filtered in from the deck above. A sliver of awning was visible through the grate, moving slightly with the slow roll of the ship. The hold itself ran the length of the vessel and was crowded with barrels, wooden crates, and bolts of brightly colored fabric.

Hafryn lay curled only a few feet away, face bloodied and pale. He'd been stripped of his sword and daggers, but to Danil's relief, his breathing was sound. Danil carefully rolled him over, squeezing his shoulder when he didn't stir. "Hafryn," he whispered.

The wolf moaned.

"He'll be fine."

Danil jolted in surprise.

Viren leaned at his ease against one of the nearby crates. Without his councilor robes, the Eyrie Keeper could be mistaken for Hafryn's older brother. They certainly dressed the same, right down to the style of leather boots and the way they carried a sword on their right hip. Danil eyed him with dislike.

"You were behind the attacks after all," Danil snarled as he moved to stand in front of Hafryn's unconscious form, fists clenched.

The councilor regarded him with cool indifference. "I assure you, custodian, no contract under my Keeping lies unfulfilled."

Why take us, then? Danil wondered. He had little sense of where they were headed, but already he could feel his connection to Kailon stretching thin.

The ship seemed to rock slightly as if adjusting to a new weight. Voices called out in greeting.

"Ah," Viren said as the hatch leading to the deck eventually opened. He smiled. "It would be for the best if you didn't fuss, Danil."

A handful of Eyrie guards clattered down the ladder. Terrified, Danil spread his feet in preparation for a fight, all too aware that Hafryn remained helpless behind him.

A young woman then made her way into the hold, and in the streaming sunlight Danil could make out the blue-tipped wings of an owl Trueform. Like Hafryn and Viren, the woman was red-haired and lightly freckled, though her eyes were coldly dark.

"My personal enchanter," Viren said by way of introduction. "Your loyalty to your wolf is admirable, Danil, but I should warn you that Merlias is not known for her patience."

The enchanter gave a poisonous smile. She wove a symbol into the air, and with a thundering heart, Danil saw it float past him to settle over Hafryn's prone form.

Merlias twisted her fingers.

A sudden rictus of pain overcame Hafryn's features. He convulsed, boots scuffing upon the wooden deck.

"What are you doing—stop!" Danil cried, throwing himself over his friend in a fruitless attempt to shield him. The crystal about his neck flared angry red.

"I seek only your word, Danil." Viren's voice was disarmingly mild. "No custodian tricks."

Hafryn convulsed again. The whites of his eyes showed, and a horrible wet sound came from his lungs as he struggled for breath.

"You have it," Danil choked out, frantic. "My word as custodian!"

Viren motioned to two guards, who roughly hauled Danil from Hafryn. "We've made our point, Merlias."

The young woman pouted slightly. "Yes, my lord." She made a cutting motion. Hafryn turned slackly unconscious once more.

"Curse you," Danil hissed, eyes stinging. His captors dragged him forward, where Viren stood with his hands clasped behind his back.

"Now your hand, if you please, custodian," Viren requested.

The guards gave Danil no chance to resist, forcing open his fist to reveal the golden House glyph of Corros.

Smiling thinly, Merlias spun a new enchantment over it. Sharp cold bit into Danil's skin. The House glyph suddenly dimmed like a banked fire, and a new glyph made of black lines and hard edges perched atop it.

Danil wrenched his hand free, gasping. The cold throbbed all the way to his elbow.

"Nicely done, Merlias," Viren commended. "The dragon prince is far too covetous to not add extra safeguards to his glyph. This way, Danil, he certainly won't find us."

The crystal was an angry murmuring in the back of Danil's mind. "I thought tampering with House glyphs was anathema to all Amasians," he uttered, shaking slightly.

"Indeed, but you were never part of the House of Corros," Viren replied, voice impersonal. "Not in a way that matters."

"That's not for you to decide," he snarled.

The Eyrie councilor gave another indifferent shrug. "Two custodians under one House can make even rational people nervous. But you should concern yourself with the here and now, custodian."

Danil's eyes narrowed. "Such as how Roldaer can now walk into Kailon at whim?"

Viren said, "That is hardly an Eyrie concern."

The councilor was far too astute to ignore the consequences of magi taking control of Kailon's leylines. "You're lying," Danil spat back. The crystal raged an angry red against his chest.

Viren's gaze settled on it, green eyes acquisitive. "It's a first crystal, isn't it?"

"What?"

"It was...resistant to removal." Viren looked mildly nonplussed. "We'd assumed the crystal was given to you by our dragon prince, but now I suspect otherwise."

Merlias released a low chuckle. "It should be easy takings now, my lord."

Viren smiled. "By all means, then, Merlias."

The guards tightened their grip on Danil's arms when he made to pull away. The crystal blackened ominously as Merlias reached for it. She paused, cautious. After a moment she withdrew her hand with a frustrated snarl.

Viren appeared delighted. "You may prove useful yet, Danil." He signaled to another guard, who strode to a nearby barrel and scooped out a cup of water. He tossed it in Hafryn's face.

Hafryn stirred, coughing, and was wrenched roughly to his feet before he could gather his bearings. Awareness filled his eyes as he took in the Eyrie holding Danil captive. Breath ragged, he snarled, "I never took you for stupid, Viren."

"Nor I you, cousin," Viren replied. He made casual steps toward Hafryn. "But I am disappointed you fell for such an obvious trap."

Hafryn bared his teeth in a humorless laugh. "You mean at the inn."

Danil threw him a startled look. His friend was thin-lipped and pale, trembling between the guards who held him, but his green eyes were sharply furious.

"The trinket box, Danil," Viren supplied. "Though for a time I thought you'd never discover it."

It still made little sense, until Danil remembered the dangerous red glyph hidden from ordinary sight. His eyes widened slightly.

Viren smirked. "Yes, we are quite aware of your skills, *videre*."

Hafryn sagged a little between the men gripping his arms. "Should have known you'd overheard Freyna, but you never let on," he said bitterly.

"The High Council's decision did force my hand, but first I had to be sure," Viren said with an eloquent shrug. "There have been only two *videre* since the time of Aramanth. Both could discern beyond the normal."

Danil shook his head. "That trinket box—do you even know what the hidden glyph does?"

"It's an Eyrie relic from before the Great War," Viren replied. "Owned by an enchanter, I believe, who had an apprentice with a liking for thievery. He did not steal again."

"You could have killed us all," Hafryn argued.

"Only if the custodian lacked the skills we need." Viren regarded Danil with detached interest. "You can't know what the Great War cost Eyrie, Danil. We paid a higher price than any other House when Kaul stole power from our great lodestone." His gaze hardened as it lowered to the crystal about Danil's neck. "As I'm sure you're aware, much of the leylines that now run under the deadlands belong to Eyrie."

Danil set his jaw. "Leylines can't be owned."

Smiling, Viren said, "A quaint assessment, custodian. We should discuss it at length sometime. But more salient is that our enchanters fought to stop Kaul from taking the lodestone from our great repository. In losing the battle, many of our glyphs were taken as well. We have spent centuries rebuilding our power, borrowing glyphs from other Houses."

"Stealing," Hafryn muttered, mouth tight. "Or as payment for murder and disorder."

"Doing as we must, exile," Merlias countered with a cold smile. Her fingers jerked as if with the desire to form a new enchantment.

"It's as Merlias says." Viren signaled her away. "However, not all Eyrie believe our glyphs are lost."

Danil frowned. "What does this have to do with us?"

"Why, I want you to search Eyrie's great repository for our lost glyphs, Danil. My enchanters trust that simply by inscribing them once again, the glyphs will return to our people."

Eyebrows raised, Danil said, "If enchanters can't find them, what makes you think I can? Maybe the stories about glyphs being returned are just that—tales sung to children and fools about faded glory."

A low hiss came from Merlias as she paced behind him. He tracked her steps on the boards.

Viren smiled. "I have sensed a power within the repository. Something yet remains where the lodestone once sat. That is where your strange abilities will prove useful."

"And if I can't do what you want?" Dani asked.

Viren glanced meaningfully at Merlias, who had slowed to a halt behind Hafryn. She looked ready to gut him, or worse. Danil knew there was worse.

The Eyrie councilor smiled benignly. "It's in everyone's best interest that you do."

L eft alone in the hold a short time later, Hafryn collapsed against a crate with a grimace. He gripped his side in obvious pain, sweat peppering his forehead.

Danil hurriedly filled a cup of water from the nearby barrel and took it to him. "How bad is it?" he whispered. The shadow of two guards was visible from the grate above them, close enough to hear every word.

"Give me a moment, *fala*," Hafryn muttered, wincing as he stretched out his legs. He gratefully took the offered cup, taking careful sips.

Nervous energy thrumming through him, Danil took a new glance about the hold. Their only escape, it seemed, would be through the hatch.

Setting the cup down, Hafryn ran his gaze over Danil's face. He reached up to run gentle fingers over a cut above Danil's eye, before tilting his chin to examine the swelling of his left cheek.

"Nothing's broken," Danil murmured.

Relief showed in Hafryn's face. "Same here, I expect. Thugs though they are, the Eyrie are far too exacting to inflict injuries that may later inconvenience them." He glanced about the hold grimly. "They need us relatively mobile."

Danil opened his palm to examine the black glyph more closely. Underneath, the symbol of Sonnen's House grew paler still, turning white like an old scar.

Hafryn cursed softly. "Viren's enchanter must be a glyph-breaker. Their talents are...unsavory to most folk."

Danil supposed it was hardly a surprise, then, that Merlias seemed so good at her task. Curling his hand into a fist, he wondered, "What if Sonnen thinks we just left Corros?"

"He'd know better. Elania, too. At the very least, we would have sent word before wrangling Griff into flying us back to Kailon."

"We should never have left in the first place," Danil murmured, despairing. Kailon lay unprotected and vulnerable, and now even more exposed to magi greed.

Hafryn leaned forward to grip the back of his neck. "This isn't your fault, *fala*." He squeezed gently. "Were it not for you, Kailon would have already fallen."

Danil knew that Magus Brianna would have inflicted terror across the lands had her plans succeeded. But that hardly freed him of his responsibilities as custodian now. The leylines trusted him to keep them safe.

Shaking his head to clear it, Danil asked, "How far is it to the repository?"

"It'll take weeks to navigate the river," Hafryn muttered. He squinted up through the grate. "Judging by the speed of this ship, we'll be at the Eyrie border in a few days."

But the border was weeks from Corros. "The ship is magicked?" Danil asked.

Hafryn nodded grimly. "They often are—the current is too fierce without it."

That explained why Danil felt Kailon rapidly drawing further and further away. "We need to get off this ship, Hafryn."

Eyes on the grate above them, Hafryn promised, "We will."

～

FIVE GUARDS TOOK to monitoring them from within the hold.

Seated beside Hafryn, Danil eyed them with obvious dislike, wondering if Viren had sent them down in light of their earlier conversation. Such precautions seemed unnecessary, considering Hafryn was unable to so much as stagger to the privy pot without assistance.

Danil resisted the urge to watch the ghostly wolf Trueforms as they ranged about the hold. Like Hafryn's wolf, they were russet red and green-eyed, and Danil abruptly realized that, together with the owls, he'd not seen any other type of Trueform among the Eyrie. He wondered if they were heading for a land solely of predators, or if he'd only been privy to the House's warrior caste.

As the day dragged on, the slosh of water against the hull lulled Danil's senses. Hafryn was a warm, heavy weight against his side, his breaths deep and steady as if in sleep. His Trueform rested its head on Danil's thigh, ears pricked as it tracked the pacing of the other wolves.

Careworn and hungry, Danil judged it was well past midday based on the angled stream of light cutting into the hold.

A sudden rap, like a butt of a staff urgently hitting the

deck above, echoed in the hold. The hatch slammed open, and Merlias jumped down and motioned quickly to the guards.

Hafryn stirred.

Before Danil could move, two men yanked him up and dragged him toward the back of the hold. He heard a scuffle and grunt of pain as Hafryn was hauled after him.

Merlias banged her fist against the wall. It gave way to a small compartment.

"What's going on?" Danil asked frantically as the guards dragged him inside.

The ship rocked slightly as if adjusting to a new weight. Unfamiliar voices, muffled by the wood, announced themselves as members of the Corros harbor guard.

Hafryn gave a pale, sweaty grin. "A search party, *fala*. Just as we expected."

Sneering, Merlias signaled to one of the guards, who kicked the back of Hafryn's leg.

As Hafryn staggered to his knees, the guard his head wrenched back and set a dagger against his throat.

"Don't—!" Danil gasped, fighting to reach him.

"Quietly, custodian," Merlias purred, taking a slow circle about Hafryn. "A sound from either of you and he dies. Understood?"

Danil nodded desperately.

Smiling, Merlias motioned for the guards to drag Hafryn into the compartment, blade still held at his throat. In the tight confines, Danil scarcely dared to breathe.

Merlias struck the wooden wall again, and the compartment closed about them.

Danil watched through a tiny crack as the enchanter climbed back through the hatch, her voice bright as she called out a greeting.

A short time later, a newcomer climbed down into the hold, and Danil recognized the somberly dressed garb and dour expression of the young man.

Griff...

One of the guards clamped his hand over Danil's mouth.

The blue dragon stalked the length of the hold, idly checking some of the crates. Viren climbed down the ladder. He tucked his hands behind his back, green eyes amused as he tracked Griff's wandering path.

"I must say, Councilor," Griff said as he continued his inspection. "I'm surprised to see you gone from Corros."

"My duties with the council ended with the vote." Viren smiled placidly. "I yearn for the High Reaches of Eyrie, as do many of my people."

Griff returned to the ladder. "Of course." He put a hand on the rail and wavered. "But you can see that timing of your absence is unexpected. It coincides with the disappearance of the human custodian, whom you had promised to protect."

Through the tiny crack, Danil saw Viren's mouth twitch.

"The human didn't get what he desired from the High Council." He shrugged eloquently. "I don't blame him for leaving. My people were released from their duty the moment he left the citadel."

Griff nodded, mouth tightening slightly as he gazed about the hold once more. "And you have no idea where Danil may have gone?"

"Ask my cousin, Griffin," Viren said. "Unless Hafryn's gone from Corros as well?" He affected a look of mild concern.

"They're both missing," Griff conceded.

"Ah, well, it appears where one goes the other will follow."

Griff nodded, expression closed. "Indeed. Very well—I apologize for slowing your journey, councilor."

"Not at all," Viren said, motioning for Griff to climb the ladder before following. "You're most welcome to some refreshments."

"Another time, councilor."

The hatch thumped closed behind them.

Danil tracked the dragon's path across the deck. A short while later, the ship rocked again, marking Griff's departure. From the corner of his eye, Danil saw the Eyrie guard lower the blade from Hafryn's neck.

"Well, that's that," Hafryn muttered.

Danil couldn't hide his dismay.

23

Three long days passed in the hold.

For the most part, Danil and Hafryn were left at peace, their guards content to stay nearest to the hatch except to deliver surprisingly hearty meals of stews, meats, and vegetables. The reprieve did Hafryn well, with color returning to his cheeks and stiffness leaving his bones. With increasing frequency, Danil's vision shifted to see his friend's wolf Trueform pace in front of them, healthy and alert once more.

But any sort of relief at Hafryn's improvement was tempered by Viren's repeated visits. The Eyrie councilor seemed to relish in the discomfort it caused, seeking details of their exploits in Kailon and Altonas. Hafryn had no hesitation in telling the man, but it made Danil wonder what tales Tresa had imparted to the High Council, and what she'd chosen to leave out.

Other times, Viren merely sat and watched. Those visits disquieted Danil the most, with Viren's Trueform so close to his face as to blot out any other view. In such moments,

Danil pretended to sleep, muscles tense as he felt Viren's smug amusement.

At present, the councilor perched on a crate loaded with darkly glazed pottery protected with straw. He read from a packet stashed beneath his overcoat, the magelight above him dipping and swaying with the gentle rock of the ship.

Danil sat with his back against the curved bulkhead, listening to the soft hush of conversation overhead and the snap and furl of the sails. Hafryn lounged beside him, sharing a blanket thrown down by one of the sailors the day before.

The hatch opened, and a handful of Eyrie entered as Danil and Hafryn uneasily rose to their feet.

"Ah," Viren said, tucking the packet into his overcoat. He climbed down from the crate. "Time, is it?"

"Aye, my lord," one replied, a burly fellow with a balding head and owl Trueform.

"Let's not dally, then," Viren said.

Two men jostled Danil aside as others grabbed Hafryn by the arms and wrenched him up the ladder.

"What's happening?" Danil asked in alarm.

Viren made a careless wave as he climbed the ladder. "By all means join us, custodian," he said, his voice amused.

Clambering after them, Danil squinted away the brightness of midday as he stepped up onto the deck. Tall grey escarpments marked both sides of the river where the water had cut deep into the landscape. The ship moved fast against the current, and Danil turned his face to the crisp breeze, momentarily reveling in its freshness.

His attention snared at the prow, where Hafryn cut a lonesome figure against the railing. Merlias stood under the mast ten feet behind him, together with an archer who looked ready to fire at the first order. Sailors and guards alike observed Hafryn with cruel and leering amusement.

Approaching, Danil noticed Hafryn's white-knuckled grip on the railing as he stared out at the grey rocks jutting out of the water.

"What is it?" Danil murmured, confused as to why they were out here.

Hafryn shook his head minutely. "We're close," he murmured.

"To Eyrie?" Danil asked, startled.

Hafryn's mouth thinned.

"You're right, cousin," Viren observed, moving to stand beside them. The breeze tugged on the fine cloth of his cloak. "The marker for our territory lies past yon river bend. I thought it only appropriate you know the moment of your return home."

Hafryn's grip on the railing tightened.

"Of course, your dragon and his cohorts cannot enter Eyrie—not without initiating a war I'm certain few can afford."

Danil squinted. "The longer I'm gone from Kailon, the more likely Roldaer will take it for themselves. Then we'll all be at war." Eyes narrowing, he added, "What you're doing —what you've done from the outset—is to the detriment of all in Amas."

Viren raised an eyebrow. "My duty is to Eyrie. Something I expect you'd understand, Danil."

He gritted his teeth in frustration.

A pillar of stone in the center of the river pulled Danil's attention. Water swirled around its base, but Danil felt drawn to the gleaming kiandrite seated in a cradle of stone at the top of the pillar. The magi would have no hesitation harvesting the crystal, Danil thought bitterly.

A haunted look crossed Hafryn's face as they drifted past the pillar.

"Welcome home, cousin," Viren uttered smugly.

"I never thought—" Hafryn stopped, throat working.

Danil could hardly imagine the pain of returning to one's homeland when all that awaited was threats and hostility. Heart aching, he placed his hand over Hafryn's on the railing and was rewarded to see his expression smooth over.

WITH THE EYRIE border behind them, Danil and Hafryn often found themselves escorted up on deck to take in the bracing spring air. Shadowed by Merlias and her archer companion, they positioned themselves in an out of the way corner of the stern as the grey escarpments gave way to forests of pine and oak and pockets of fields. A few children played on the banks, waving as they sailed past. None of the Eyrie waved back.

Danil leaned against the railing, the breeze in his face. The current was against them, but the ship moved apace. He slid a gaze to the helmswoman, whose eyes were distant as she expertly steered the vessel past a trading boat making its way downriver. Tiny glyphs glowed on the wheel under her hand.

They continued along the river for the remainder of the day, passing skiffs and fishing boats. Most were heading for Corros to trade, others supplying the small villages and hamlets that dotted the river.

At Viren's urging, the helmswoman continued on after sunset, using lamps at the head of the ship to light the way. As the moon rose above the river, off duty Eyrie congregated at the bow of the boat to share a flagon. Each poured a dram into a tumbler and tossed it over the side before taking a mouthful themselves.

Hafryn muttered something under his breath and stalked past his armed escort to enter the hold.

Danil watched him disappear with a quizzical look and made to follow.

"They practice *dranst*," Viren said from where he stood beside the helmswoman. He indicated for Hafryn's guards to join the other Eyrie. "It's a customary drink that only adult Eyrie may partake in."

That didn't explain what irked Hafryn, however.

Viren watched his companions with amusement. "Hafryn left before his maturation ceremony."

Mouth falling open, Danil asked, "So you don't view Hafryn as an adult?"

"Exactly so." Viren smiled. "Of course, it is unlikely he would be welcome even if he'd completed the ceremony." His expression turned conciliatory. "No need to take offense for your lover—a gentle reminder of his exile is better than the alternative, no?"

Hafryn still bore the marks of their kidnapping. Danil shook his head. "I thought the cleansing ritual meant no Eyrie could hurt him."

Still smiling, Viren conceded, "It's true that attacking someone so recently cleansed is prohibited. But with sufficient cause, a Keeper can make an exception."

Eyeing him with dislike, Danil said, "In other words, you can throw aside the protection whenever you damn well please."

Amusement showed in his green eyes. "If you're wondering why I bothered at all, Danil, consider our company. Few believe Hafryn is deserving of the Eyrie name."

Danil's gaze instinctively went to Merlias, whose owl Trueform perched upon the rigging above her. She sat aloof from the other Eyrie, scowling out into the night.

"No," Viren said, following his gaze. "Merlias follows my will. Nonetheless, I couldn't risk anyone jeopardizing our mission by getting inventive."

Fighting off a shudder, Danil muttered, "Very thorough of you."

Viren smiled. "I'm glad you understand, Danil."

Gritting his teeth, Danil took his leave and followed after Hafryn into the hold. He startled to see the ghostly wolf Trueform on his haunches in the barred moonlight of the grate. Hafryn himself was curled under a blanket in the shadow of the bulkhead. Danil sat beside him with a sigh, watching how the wolf's ears were folded back as laughter filtered down from the deck.

"You're seeing my Trueform, aren't you?" Hafryn muttered with a huff, throwing back the blanket.

"I don't need to see it to know your thoughts."

Green eyes met his gaze. "You're getting good at it—seeing Trueforms," he observed grudgingly.

Danil shrugged, wondering how it could possibly help them against Viren and his bloodthirsty enchanter. "We'll need something better if we're to get out of this."

Hafryn grunted. "Or my blades. And best before we reach the repository. If you can't do what Viren demands—" He shook his head.

"Will he kill us?"

Hesitating a moment, Hafryn said, "He spoke truly about Eyrie not killing custodians, but do we really want to find out, *fala*?"

Danil released a sigh, feeling exhaustion in his bones. "We have to get back to Kailon," he murmured. "If I'm truly *videre*, it's because Kailon needs me to be, not the Eyrie."

"Viren is smart, and that makes him arrogant." Hafryn's eyes grew hooded. "We'll find our advantage."

Danil noted the weary lines about his friend's eyes. "Just being among them hurts you, doesn't it?"

A ghost of a smile pulled Hafryn's lips. "Don't fret, *fala*. It's exactly as I imagined it."

24

T he sun sat low on the horizon the following day when they docked at an Eyrie village.

A handful of locals fished from the dock and watched with wary eyes as Danil and Hafryn were ushered off the ship. With Viren at the head of the party, they followed a cobbled path that wound between stunted trees and huts made of somber grey stone. An uneasy quiet held over the village, its occupants furtive in the shadows.

The path led them into a central courtyard where a stone tower squatted like a lichen-stained toad. Dead grass pushed up through cracks in the stone. The tower's shadow seemed overlong, its black spire missing tile in places. Danil uneasily eyed the heavy door at the base of the tower, its ancient wood warped with disuse.

Viren motioned a handful of guards forward.

A burly shifter rammed his shoulder against the wooden door. It creaked and groaned under the attack. A few more shoves and it splintered apart.

Merlias entered with a number of other shifters to disappear into the gloom.

Hafryn watched on with obvious apprehension. "I thought we were going to the great repository at Reppa," he said edgily.

Viren placed hands on his hips as he peered up at the spire. "Many villages once held places of learning such as this. When Kaul attacked the great repository and took our glyphs, our learning centers suffered a similar fate." He turned to Danil, green eyes serene. "You're of no use to me if at Reppa if you cannot find the glyphs here."

Gulping, Danil knew he was scarcely ready for such a task, not when his grip on his burgeoning abilities was so tenuous.

Merlias emerged moments later to nod at Viren.

"Inside, custodian," Viren said. "Find my glyphs, and I will ensure Hafryn lives."

Brushing off the guard who made to grab his arm, Danil strode up the single step into the tower. To his surprise, the interior comprised of a hollow room that reached the full height of the building. It was empty save for a stone platform, which Danil imagined was once used for teaching younglings and would-be enchanters.

Glancing at Hafryn, Danil shifted his vision to see his Trueform pace agitatedly in front of the platform. Behind him, all but Viren's great wolf had backed up close to the entrance.

At Viren's nod, a pair of Eyrie moved up behind Hafryn. Hafryn turned to face them, his expression bland.

"By all means, Danil, take your ease," Viren said serenely.

Message received, Danil set about examining the damp walls. Moss grew in patches on the wet stone. To his growing apprehension, he spied no markings or flashes of kiandrite.

He took a slow turn about the room, desperate to buy himself time.

"Mayhap you underestimated his abilities, my lord," Merlias suggested, her voice bored.

"It does appear so," Viren replied. He motioned to the guards.

"Wait!" Danil said with hand raised as Hafryn bared his teeth in readiness for an attack. Gripping the crystal about his neck, Danil tried to calm his racing mind. The kiandrite sent him an inquisitive trill.

'*Help us,*' he begged.

It shivered against his palm.

'*Please...*'

A strange flickering passed over Danil's vision, and suddenly a ghost-like glyph floated above the platform. It cast a dark red film over the walls and floor, with spidery red tendrils reaching out in an ugly web to almost every corner of the tower. He glanced about in astonishment, but no one else seemed to notice it.

The crystal whispered urgently to him.

Danil's eyes followed the thickest line to a niche in the wall, where the blood-red web sat anchored to a set of undulating spirals. On closer examination, Danil found that each anchor point rested over similar engravings on the wall.

They're glyphs, he realized with an excited jolt. The red glyph floating above the center of the platform seemed almost to be feeding off them, draining the last remnants of kiandrite stored within.

These had to be the lost glyphs of Eyrie. But how to free them?

Danil gazed again at the thickest rope of menacing red

light. It pulsed darkly, and for a moment he smelled a fetid burning. A wrongness lay over this glyph. Strangely, it reminded him of parts of Kailon where even the leylines wouldn't go, and every instinct warned Danil not to approach.

'*Trust,*' the crystal on his chest suddenly murmured in his mind

Startled, Danil glanced down to see it aglow with vibrant hues of azure and green.

"You test my patience, custodian," Viren growled nearby.

Knowing he had little time, Danil gave his trust to the crystal and reached out with a halting breath. His fingers brushed the malevolent web.

Lightning scorched across his palm. From one heartbeat to the next, Danil felt the shattering of Merlias' glyph on his skin, along with the eradication of the last remnants of his connection to the House of Corros. He screamed in agony. He felt something drain from him like the tapping of blood from a vein.

"*Danil!*"

Hafryn caught him as he collapsed. His palm was afire with excruciating agony. The acrid stench of burning, wrongness, and death was so strong Danil could taste it.

"Great gods," Merlias breathed, wheeling about. She gave a delighted laugh.

Blinking through tears of pain, Danil looked up to see the walls alight with glyphs. There were dozens, hundreds, spanning all sides of the tower. They shone in a rainbow of colors as a radiant hum vibrated through the air.

"Remarkable. It is more beautiful than I ever imagined," Viren murmured, green eyes awestruck. About them, Eyrie stared up in slack-jawed wonder.

Crouched beside him, Hafryn seemed to care little for the vista. He gently turned Danil's hand up. An ugly, writhing mess of a red glyph blistered his palm. Hafryn swore.

Shuddering, Danil realized it was the same sullen red glyph that had held all those others under its thrall. Its wrongness sent bile to his throat. "No," he choked out. His hand trembled.

"This is just the beginning, my lord," Merlias announced grandly, all but dancing in her glee. "We must continue on to the next village and all others until Eyrie is returned to glory!"

Danil tried to stagger to his feet but had no strength. He crumpled to his knees, shaking. "You gave your word, Viren," he gasped with an effort. "The glyphs are free— grant us the same."

Drawing his gaze from the shimmering walls, Viren looked them both over contemplatively. "That was not part of our bargain, *videre.*"

Danil stared at him, miserable and shaking. In his despair, he realized Viren spoke truly—on their first day in the hold, he'd agreed to Hafryn's safety but had been tricked out of ensuring their freedom as well.

"You conniving *bastard!*" Hafryn hissed. He had one arm over Danil's shoulders, holding him close. "What more can you ask of him?"

Viren raised an eloquent eyebrow. "Can you assure me that all the glyphs of Eyrie are awakened, Hafryn? We have no way telling."

"You've got more than your blood's worth here!" Hafryn snarled.

"You're overwrought," the councilor observed with

almost courtly solicitude. He beckoned to Merlias. "Perhaps you're in need of rest to get over your understandable disappointment at this misunderstanding."

Merlias skipped to the wall to Danil's left, tracing her fingers over one glyph before traipsing to another. She paused at one made of concentric circles. "How about this one, my lord?"

Viren shook his head. "I'd prefer an enchantment whose purpose you already know, Merlias. And no permanent damage, if you will."

She stepped away from the wall with a pout. "Fine," she sighed, hands weaving.

Nauseous with fear, Danil found himself pulled close by Hafryn, head tucked under his friend's chin. He squeezed his eyes shut as he felt the enchantment spread over them.

'*Trust,*' the crystal whispered again.

The first crystal flared so bright that it burned past Danil's clenched eyelids. A boom of power swept through him, shaking him to the core.

Shouting and cries rang about the tower. Bodies fell heavily around them, and Danil opened his eyes to see Merlias among those convulsing with pain. The crystal was a throbbing beat of light against his chest as it rebounded and magnified Merlias' spell.

Hafryn looked about in astonishment. "What—?" Mouth hardening with resolve, he grabbed the fabric of Danil's tunic. "Here's our chance, *fala!*"

He hauled Danil up by main force, half carrying him through the broken doorway. Danil saw Viren blindly reach out toward them, fury on his contorted face.

The courtyard was empty as Hafryn lugged him toward the cobbled path. Danil could hardly keep his feet, gasping for breath as the pain of the glyph on his hand sharpened again. Glowering red light snaked across his flesh.

"The ship's too big for us to take," Hafryn muttered, lowering Danil at the back of a hut. The river burbled a short distance away. "I saw a few fishing skiffs as we came in —*fala*, can you make it?"

Danil pushed down the pain and acrid bile burning his throat. "I'm fine," he managed.

Looking dubious, Hafryn nonetheless nodded. At his urging, they staggered for the dock. A handful of small skiffs bobbed in the gentle waves. Hafryn pointed to one devoid of fish traps and nets. "That one."

He half carried, half dragged Danil to it and eased him down onto the wooden boards. It smelled rankly of fish and dirty bilge water, but Danil ignored it and stumbled to the tiller.

Hafryn ran the length of the dock, slicing the moorings of other skiffs and small boats.

Taking a steadying breath, Danil nervously waited for Eyrie to reveal themselves on the cobbled path, but no outcry came. The repository towered over the village. It seemed brighter somehow, no longer shadowed and looming. Danil watched Hafryn cut loose the moorings of the Viren's ship and push hard on its port side until the vessel became caught in the current.

Running along the dock, Hafryn similarly cut their own skiff free and jumped aboard. He took the tiller as the current quickly gripped the small craft. He navigated them past an unmanned boat with ease.

"Stay low, *fala*," Hafryn muttered. "We may not have much time before they shake loose of that enchantment."

Heartbeats later, movement along the bank caught Danil's eye. Viren's ghostly Trueform pushed through the reeds and settled on its haunches. It watched their journey downstream with dry bemusement. There was no activity from the village.

Danil continued to stare until the skiff rounded the bend of the river, and the wolf was lost from sight.

25

The heated glyph pulled Danil from a sweaty dream filled with burning forests, blackened rocks and a tunnel that went deep into the earth. Mouth dry, he awkwardly pushed himself up into sitting position at the prow of the skiff. His hand was a raw ache under its makeshift bandage, and he held it close to his chest as he glanced about.

Dawn turned the sky pink above the tree canopy and snow-tipped mountains. A lone deer stood on the pebbled bank to Danil's right, poised for flight as the skiff drifted silently past. Glancing at the tiller, Danil saw weariness under Hafryn's eyes, but he recognized the determined set of his friend's jaw, also. Hafryn acknowledged him with a warm look as he expertly navigated past a series of exposed rocks. They'd traveled the river for the entire night, knowing that to stop would surely mean capture.

Already other skiffs and boats were on the water, carrying goods for trade upstream or setting out to fish in the estuaries and streams feeding off the river. Their occupants studied Danil and Hafryn with unwelcoming or cautious eyes. Hafryn seemed intent on ignoring them, and Danil knew there was no avoiding being seen. Regardless, their journey could come as no surprise to Viren and his party. There was only one place the custodian would go.

Home, Danil thought with a sudden yearning for the deep gullies and murmuring leylines of Kailon.

But with the foul glyph on his palm, Danil was no longer sure of his welcome. There was a wrongness to it that made him loathe to enter the sacred groves.

The crystal glowed apologetic yellow against his tunic. Danil glanced at it with a mix of confusion and betrayal, wondering if it had known what would happen when it directed him to touch the malignant red web. But doing so had released Eyrie's lost glyphs, and the crystal had been the sole instigator of their escape in the moments afterward.

Danil lifted the crystal with his uninjured hand. It released a cautious trill as if it, too, was uncertain of belonging. That softened Danil a little, and he stroked its smooth edges. The crystal warmed to pink with striations of gold and something settled within Danil. No matter what lay on his palm, they had to return to Kailon. The leylines were counting on him to keep them safe. The crystal changed to a resolute blue.

"Here," Hafryn abruptly said in the quiet, leaning forward to take Danil's wrist. "Let me see, *fala*." He gently upturned Danil's injured hand and unwound the makeshift bandage.

The skin about the glyph appeared blistered and raw, but thankfully showed no lines of infection. The glyph itself flooded the skiff with surly red light. It writhed when Danil wiggled his fingers.

Hafryn dabbed the wound clean, careful not to touch the glyph. A deep frown marred his forehead.

"It's of Kaul's making, isn't it?" Danil asked, feeling an unnamable dread just from looking upon it.

Hafryn's mouth tightened. "Not my field of expertise, I'm afraid. But from the way you described things back at the village—" He stopped to nod grimly.

"It destroyed Merlias' glyph," Danil muttered as a rush of misery gripped him. "Sonnen's, too." The loss of the latter he felt keenly. He'd only been part of the House of Corros for a few months, but such belonging had proven a source of comfort in the recent upheavals of his life.

Danil stared uneasily at the hard, spiked lines of the glyph, wishing that will alone could see it gone. He dreaded what would happen if he inadvertently activated it.

The glyph darkened with malevolent knowing.

Suddenly, a roar of flames filled his ears, and for a moment Danil saw the mine shaft leading down to the Temple of Kaul. An angry, primal beat drummed through his veins.

"Danil!" Hafryn hissed in alarm.

Danil recoiled, momentarily dizzy.

Hafryn gripped his shoulder, eyes wide and terrified. "You started to go...somewhere."

Sucking in a tight, cloying breath, Danil waited for the thundering in his ears to diminish. The glyph returned to a brooding red.

"Let's keep this covered, eh?" Hafryn said, shaken. He bandaged the wound once again with strips of his tunic. "At least until folk more knowledgeable than us can free you of it."

Setting his aching hand on his knee, Danil said, "We have to get back to Kailon, Hafryn." There was something about the Temple of Kaul; something important. The crystal murmured urgently, glowing dark blue in agreement.

"We will," Hafryn promised, giving Danil's shoulder a final squeeze. He returned to the tiller, gazing upstream where small rapids glittered in the early morning light. A handful of boats navigated the river, but none drew close to them with any sort of intent.

It reminded Danil of their other problem. "Can Viren's party get ahead of us?"

Hafryn shook his head, his troubled expression easing slightly. "The mountain passes are too difficult to travel with any sort of speed." His eyes swept the forest canopy. "Wings are another matter."

Danil eyed the trees nervously for owls. He feared what would happen if they were captured once more. "Viren was going to torture you again."

Hafryn snorted. "The Eyrie aren't driven by sentiment. Viren's no exception."

"But you are."

Hafryn's attention flicked back to him, eyes wide with surprise. "I suppose I am," he mused. "A consequence of living outside my House, I expect."

Danil suspected it was more than that. Based in recent experience, the Eyrie seemed a wholly suspicious and cruel people. Hafryn, however secretive at times, was fiercely loyal and protective of those he loved.

Hafryn's mouth pulled downwards as he admitted, "I'd hoped Viren would surprise me. Stupid, even after all this time." He rubbed his eyes.

"Anyone who calls you kin—it can have a powerful hold," Danil murmured.

Hafryn's throat worked. "Aye, despite all common sense and past misdeeds." He shook himself with obvious effort. "I've no regrets for being exiled, *fala*. Not when it has brought me to you."

Warmth coiled in Danil's belly. From the moment he fled the magi in Farin, he'd lurched from one unknown to another. But his one constant sat before him, together with his unlikely friendship with Sonnen, Elania, and Blutark.

"Your crystal is glowing, *fala*."

It swirled with dots of light against Danil's chest. Startled, he raised it high. Specks of orange light danced along the length of the skiff like floating embers from a fire. Under the bandage, his palm grew hot.

"Danil?" Freyna's startled, disembodied voice came from the crystal.

He almost dropped it, fingers scrabbling for purchase.

Hafryn leaned close. "Freyna!" He threw Danil an astonished glance. "How in the gods did you find us?"

"I believe you found me, my dears." Amusement threaded her voice. "There are many searching for you."

"We're in Eyrie," Danil said. He cupped the crystal in both hands.

"Eyrie!" Freyna gasped. "Sonnen had his suspicions, but—"

"We need help if you can muster it," Hafryn interrupted. "There's no telling how long we have before Viren's party are upon us again."

Danil glanced again at the forest sprawling close to the banks.

"Of course." A rustling sound echoed about the skiff, and suddenly a new voice rumbled from the crystal.

"Hafryn. Danil," Sonnen rumbled. "It is good to hear you both well."

"Of a sort," Hafryn replied dryly. He squeezed Danil's shoulder. "We're on the Orin River, about a half day from the great rapids."

"I know the place. We will come for you," Sonnen promised.

The tension in Danil's spine eased a little.

"Danil, how are you doing this?" Freyna asked, curiosity coloring her voice. "Communicating through kiandrite is a master enchanter's skill."

"I don't think I'm the one doing it—not intentionally, at least," Danil admitted, fearful that it was the glyph at work.

Hafryn shared a similar thought. "It's easier if we show you what's happened. But we must make for Kailon. Freyna, are you well enough to meet us there?"

"Perfectly so, my dears."

Sonnen gave a low growl. "She exaggerates and shall remain in bed. I'll send Elania in her stead."

An indelicate snort rang out. "So I'm too frail to leave my sickbed but well enough not to need my carer, hmm?"

Sonnen sighed, and Danil could all but imagine the dragon prince squeezing his nose in frustration. "Yes, Freyna. That is indeed what I said."

She huffed, though her tone was teasing. "Very well. I accede to your greater wisdom, dragon. My leylines are very much still in need of calming—though, Danil, you should know they stand with you."

The crystal turned a sallow green as a jealous grumble entered Danil's mind.

"I'm honored, Freyna," he managed, then gave the crystal a gentle squeeze.

"As does Corros," Sonnen added, unaware of the crystal's mood. "No matter the High Council's decision."

Danil shared a glance with Hafryn. "I decide Kailon's fate, not the High Council of Amas."

Hafryn gave him an approving wink.

"Oh, my dear, we already know," Freyna said. "It is good to hear you say it, though."

"If the winds are kind, we should be with you tomorrow," Sonnen said. "Hafryn, can we expect trouble?"

"With Viren? Always." They both glanced upriver. "We'll not be retaken, however," Hafryn vowed.

"There will be an accounting for what he has done," Sonnen assured. "In the meantime, keep an eye on the sky."

"And a hand upon the blade," Hafryn promised.

26

Buoyed by the prospect of rescue, Danil and Hafryn continued down the river as the day turned to night, passing the occasional village and farmholds interspersed between the grey escarpments and forest.

Morning came, and Danil took his turn at the tiller as Hafryn caught a rare moment's rest curled up on the flat-bottomed prow. The sun made the freckles over Hafryn's nose starkly evident, wisps of red hair loosened from his braid to be pushed about in the crisp air. Even in sleep, Hafryn held their one weapon close, a rusted fishing knife they'd found abandoned under a plank of loose wood. Shifting his vision, Danil saw the wolf similarly curled up, nose to tail, and he admired them both.

In truth, Danil was similarly dead on his feet. He could scarcely sleep, not with the heated glyph riding like a dark shadow in the back of his mind.

A flash of blue flitting between the pines on the left bank caught his eye. With a shock of dread, Danil recognized the ghostly owl Trueform.

He reached down to grip Hafryn's shoulder. "Hafryn," he murmured. "Merlias' Trueform is in the trees."

The wolf shifter was alert and upright in a heartbeat.

A raucous roar came from behind them, and Danil spun to see a fleet of skiffs making their way down the river. Upon the foremost boat, Viren stood ominously on the prow, hands clasped behind his back as the wind whipped his cloak about. Other Eyrie leaned over the sides or clung to the rigging, grins visible in the distance.

At some unseen signal, owls launched into the air.

Hafryn moved to the bow of the skiff, rusted knife in his clenched fist. Heart racing, Danil quickly worked to rip free the bandage about his hand.

Hafryn glanced back at him, scowling. "Don't—what are you *doing?*"

"I honestly have no idea," Danil muttered, hurrying to join him. He certainly wasn't going to see them captured again, not without a fight.

He looked up to see the owls abruptly scatter.

A great shadow passed over them, and Danil saw blue scales and a long, sinuous neck. The air about them billowed and gusted as powerful wings whomped.

"It's Griff!" Danil shouted in relief.

The blue dragon roared so loudly Danil had to cover his ears.

Hafryn climbed the railing, cheering as the fleet tacked wildly to avoid a massive ball of flame that struck the water with a violent, boiling hiss. Viren quickly retreated from view, the lead skiff yawing hard to turn about. Griff raked powerful talons across the bow of one boat slow to flee, sending its occupants diving into the water.

Danil whooped in delight.

Griff launched back into the air with a single flap of his

wings and swung about. Releasing a tremendous roar, he came barreling down toward Danil and Hafryn.

Hafryn stepped down from the railing. "*Fala—*"

Danil had no time to brace. A tremendous weight slammed into the skiff, and suddenly he was catapulted into the river. Frothing water churned about him as he was pulled down by the current. Broken planks of wood and rope tangled about him. Danil pushed to the surface, gasping. The air rang with an enraged dragon's screams.

Griff flapped above the remains of the skiff, hissing and snarling as he scored the deck with powerful talons. The blue dragon ripped apart the mast where Hafryn had last stood.

"Hafryn!" Danil screamed, fighting the current.

The blue dragon swiveled his powerful head toward Danil. A heartbeat later, Griff launched across the water and landed atop him. Powerful talons snared Danil and forced him deep underwater. His back struck the muddy bottom, and Danil thrashed, air forced from his lungs from the immense pressure of the dragon's grip.

Above the frothing water, a red wolf launched onto the dragon. Griff's enraged bellow reverberated into the depths as Hafryn scrabbled to find purchase on the dragon's scales. The wolf sunk powerful jaws into the meat of Griff's shoulder. Griff raked at Hafryn to tear him loose.

Danil grabbed a rock and smashed it against the dragon's talons. Through the blurred surface, he saw blood hit the water before Hafryn was hurtled across the river.

Bubbles released from Danil's mouth as he screamed. He stretched out his hand toward the surface and felt something *push* through him.

In a blast of poisonous red light, Griff was shunted backwards.

Lungs burning, Danil kicked up to the surface. Bursting free, he gasped, sucking in great gulps of air, and thrashed about. Hafryn floated face down only a few feet away. Danil splashed toward him, turning him about to see blood covering his front.

A flash of blue caught Danil's eye as Griff crashed downstream. The dragon seemed disorientated, momentarily blinded as he flailed about in the water.

A heartbeat later, a golden dragon landed on top of him with a wild screech. Griff floundered, trying to launch with a desperate splash but Sonnen had him by the neck. They bit and tore at each other with shocking intensity.

Coughing, Danil kicked for the bank, hauling Hafryn's unconscious form with him. Beyond the fighting dragons, Viren's fleet of skiffs continued to retreat, with only one boat pausing to collect those who'd been tossed into the water.

Hands suddenly reached down from the bank, and for a terrifying moment, Danil thought Merlias had them. He blindly struck out, only for his wrist to be firmly snared. Flinching, he looked up to find Patril, the commander of Altonas, together with a dozen crow shifters.

"Patril?" he choked.

"Steady, custodian," Patril said as she heaved him up the rocks. Two men moved quickly to get Hafryn out of the water. "We have you both."

Four of her archers lingered on the bank, bolts trained on the fleeing Eyrie skiffs as another crow rolled Hafryn over and pressed a finger to his throat. She quickly set her hands to the deep claw marks raked across Hafryn's chest as an enchantment burst forth. Danil desperately clasped Hafryn's hand, fearful of how deep the wounds were now that the river wasn't washing away the worst of the bleeding.

His crystal sang loud enough for Patril to give it a sharp look.

Moments later, Hafryn heaved in a strangled cough as his eyes snapped open.

Danil choked out a relieved cry. He pressed their foreheads together, eyes stinging.

"Steady, now," the healer warned.

"Hardly a scratch," Hafryn rasped with a weak smile. He tried to rise but grimaced in pain.

Upstream, Sonnen forced Griff into his human form. The blue dragon shifter appeared unconscious as Sonnen hurled him onto the bank.

Blinking away tears, Danil sucked in exhausted breaths. "Why would Griff do this?" he wondered aloud. "Why fight off the Eyrie if only to attack us himself?"

Hafryn gave a new groan, although it was laced with cynical realization. "Because that's the only way he could be sure you wouldn't get away. You've escaped two assassinations already, *fala*."

Danil stared down at him with confusion, wondering if Hafryn had injured his head, also.

Patril quirked an eyebrow. "Sonnen has had us follow Griff for some time now."

But that made no sense, either.

"Don't you get it, *fala*?" Hafryn pressed bitterly. "Griff's been trying to kill you for weeks."

27

A copse of pine trees gave them sanctuary away from the river. Patril sent her crows to scout the area about the camp and upstream for any sign of Viren and his followers. The branches overhead creaked and sighed in the breeze, with a crow perched in the foliage to watch over them. Patril herself walked a slow patrol about the camp, dark eyes intent.

Still, Danil couldn't shake the rush of fear at how close he and Hafryn had come to capture and death. Rattled, he had to accept that his journey into Amas had been nothing like he'd expected. There was so much intrigue, vendettas and deals within deals that he wondered how the kingdom wasn't at war with itself. His only hope was that Arlyn hadn't reached a similar conclusion. A fractured, discordant Amas would only make Roldaer bolder.

Hafryn lay stretched out on a cloak amidst the dry pine needles, his stomach and chest exposed as the healer continued her work. Small iridescent glyphs dotted Hafryn's skin.

To Danil's relief, the bleeding had stopped, but the long

wounds courtesy of Griff's talons appeared raw and painful. For his part, Hafryn remained still and white-lipped, though he complained bitterly at the loss of the fishing knife to the river. Danil suspected his friend had spent long, quiet moments imagining how he'd use it should he ever face Viren again.

With a sigh, the healer sat back. "You'll scar handsomely, my friend." She sounded pleased with her work.

Grabbing a clean tunic given to him by one of the crows, Hafryn tipped Danil a rakish wink. "As long as you agree, *fala*."

Danil ignored Hafryn and instead addressed the healer. "Can he travel?"

"By morning, I expect, if he doesn't do anything stupid," she said as she tucked the small vial of iridescent paint away into a pack. "Injuries inflicted by a dragon are the most difficult to remedy. Even your master healer friend would find it a struggle."

"You mean Elania?" Danil asked in surprise.

The healer merely nodded and pointed to his hand. "May I attend you, custodian?"

Curling up his hand, Danil resisted the urge to hide the glyph behind his back. "I'm not sure a healing can fix this," he admitted grimly.

"There's a darkness about you, but I don't think it's of your own making," she observed calmly with a tilted head.

Danil stared at her, wondering if her lack of disquiet was related somehow to her crow heritage. During their adventures in Altonas, he'd discovered crows were unflinching and resolute no matter the danger.

Her Trueform perched on her shoulder, gazing back at him with beady black eyes.

"I, too, can sense the wrongness," Sonnen said, stepping

away from where Griff sat bound and surly on the ground. Two crow enchanters guarded the blue dragon shifter, having cleared a circle about him in the pine needles to etch warding glyphs. Shifting his vision, Danil saw Griff's Trueform stalk outside the ring, unable to enter.

"Might as well show them, *fala*," Hafryn said, gingerly climbing to his feet.

Danil nervously raised his palm. Blackened blisters scored the edges of the glyph, and the glyph itself radiated such heat that Danil wondered if his companions could feel it.

Sonnen's eyes widened slightly in recognition. "It would be most unwise to place a healing enchantment over Danil's injuries," he said to the crow healer. "Herbs and unguents only, if you please."

She bowed and stepped away to gather the necessary materials.

"You know what it is," Hafryn surmised with a mix of relief and trepidation.

Sonnen gripped Danil's wrist to tilt the glyph toward the dappled sunlight spilling through the pines. "Indeed. You must tell me how you acquired it, Danil," he said urgently. "Spare no detail."

Heart racing, he and Hafryn recounted the events that had transpired since their capture. Danil took pains to remember all that had happened in the tower that had been beyond his friend's ability to see.

Sonnen looked troubled at how the crystal had played its part. "We can only hope that Kailon's leylines know things that we do not." He examined the sharp, pulsating lines more closely. "It has taken my House glyph," he noted somberly.

Swallowing against a sudden ache, Danil whispered, "Yes."

Despite how he'd not found much sense of belonging in Corros itself, Danil mourned the House glyph as a symbol of his unlikely friendship with the dragon prince.

Hafryn shifted anxiously on his feet. "Sonnen, what can you tell us about the damned thing?"

Sonnen gave Danil's wrist a gentle squeeze before releasing him. "In the catacomb libraries at Corros, there are numerous references to Kaul's magi-generals—they bore this very glyph."

Confirmation that it was one of Kaul's workings came hardly as a surprise to Danil, not when the glyph emanated such foulness.

"To what purpose?" he asked with an effort.

"There are writings by enchanters who fought in the Great War. They tell of firemages who set about burning the forests that grew above the leylines. Kaul's magi-generals somehow harvested the dead kiandrite released with the ash."

"Ash? Firemages?" Hafryn threw Danil a startled look. "*Fala*, your visions."

Sonnen looked between them, a low rumble in his chest.

"I've seen Kailon burn," Danil admitted to the dragon prince. "First in Corros, and then since getting the glyph, I've had dreams and visions of the entrance to Kaul's temple." The crystal on his chest was a beseeching hum in his mind. "We have to go down there."

"Are you certain that's a good idea?" Hafryn asked, caution in his green eyes. "Entering Kaul's former domain when you bear his glyph doesn't seem wise." He glanced at Sonnen hopefully. "Unless you can remove it?"

Sonnen shook his head. "I fear what would happen if we try."

Danil swallowed, rubbing his uninjured hand over the crystal. "I have to trust that the leylines have a purpose driving all of this."

Sonnen studied him contemplatively for a time. He nodded. "Very well. We shall make the journey to Kailon."

Relief left Danil almost dizzy.

"And preferably before Viren decides to return," Hafryn added with a grim look toward the river where it sparkled between the pines. "But what about Griff?" Hafryn asked.

They all turned to stare at the blue dragon. Griff raised his eyes to glare back with haughty contempt.

Danil shook his head. "I still don't understand how you figured out Griff was behind the assassins."

"Griff's activities of late have been unusual," Sonnen started.

Hafryn gave a derisive snort. "You mean he volunteered to help find us when we went missing from Corros."

Sonnen grunted in acknowledgement. "That he also flew Elania to Corros was irregular. I'd hoped it was out of genuine concern for Freyna, but when he offered his aid in the search for you, my suspicions grew. Griff has never been one to care deeply for others." He shook his head. "Patril was happy to lend some of her crows to the task of keeping an eye on him. She sent word of Griff being hereabouts last night."

"We're fortunate she did," Hafryn muttered, giving the commander a bow as she continued her patrol about the camp.

Patril paused and inclined her head. "My people in Altonas haven't forgotten what you've done for us, Custodian Danil."

Flushing slightly, Danil replied, "I'm grateful to you." Without her warning to Sonnen, he was sure he would have lost Hafryn to the river and likely died himself.

Patril smiled and continued her patrol.

Danil thought back to Griff's mad fury as he tried to kill them. His skin pebbled, and he rubbed his arms briskly. "I don't know how we could have offended Griff so much in the first place."

Sonnen raised an eyebrow. "Shall we ascertain his reasoning?"

Hafryn glowered across the camp. "By all means."

They made their way to where Griff sat within the enchanters' circle. The blue dragon didn't bother to rise, gazing up at them with disdain.

Sonnen crouched until they were at eye level. "You have betrayed me, Griffin. And your people as well."

Griff sneered but said nothing.

"What insult could Danil have possibly perpetrated to inspire your rage, hmm?" Sonnen pressed. "Or is your hatred of humans so deep that you cannot see Danil for the man he is?"

That irritated Griff into speaking. "I couldn't care less who and what Danil is," he spat. "It's what you plan to do with him, Sonnen, that forced my hand!"

Tiny twin flames showed in the dragon prince's eyes. "Explain it to me."

"Two custodians," Griff spat. "Two lands! You might have everyone at Corros fooled, Sonnen, but I see your goal. You want all of Amas for yourself. And you'll use some fake custodian to achieve it!"

Sonnen's mouth parted, the flame abruptly vanishing from his eyes. "You—*what*?"

"I see how you spend all your days on the deadlands,

how your eyes are always turned beyond our borders," Griff snarled. "I'm not the only one who thinks your ways have become strange to us." He glared at the dragon prince. "I see the path you're taking. Kaul also didn't will himself into power; he took it."

"That is not my purpose in Kailon, Griff," Sonnen said, his expression troubled. "Danil is part of my House only until he creates his own."

Danil threw the dragon prince an astonished look. "I can make my own House?" he blurted.

Rumbling low in his chest, Sonnen nodded.

Hafryn huffed. "You didn't think Kailon would become part of Corros, did you, *fala*?"

Resisting the urge to inspect his bandaged hand, Danil admitted, "I don't know what to think."

Griff bared his teeth in a mocking grin. "You believe Sonnen will give you a choice, custodian? Even now, he covets your power for himself!"

Flames returned to Sonnen's eyes. "And what was your intent with Freyna? She would be well had you not sent an assassin to attack her."

"An unfortunate mistake," Griff hissed, although his eyes lowered in shame. He turned heated eyes back to Danil. "Amas would be better off without you. You know nothing of our ways, human. It makes you stupid and easy to control. The deadlands should have chosen another; one not so clearly eager to bow down to Sonnen's machinations. Better that you die than allow him to destroy Amas."

Danil stared, wondering if that was true.

Hafryn snorted. "You were also within the Temple of Kaul when Magus Brianna was defeated. The well of kiandrite didn't choose you for a reason, Griff."

"And I'm grateful." Griff smiled humorlessly. "The

deadlands are tainted by Kaul—why else do you think the High Council was so desperate to be rid of it?"

"*What?*" Danil gasped.

It all suddenly made sense why the council had snubbed him in their rush to reach an accord with Arlyn and Roldaer. They never saw any value in Kailon to begin with.

"Let the magi have it," Griff continued, eyes shining manically. "The leylines of Amas will remain pure."

Hafryn folded his arms. "Kaul's legacy continues to poison Altonas and Eyrie—your ideas of purity are a little murky, Griff."

The blue dragon sneered dismissively.

Danil turned to Sonnen. "I have to return to Kailon now. If the High Council cares so little about what happens there, they may have given Roldaer permission to harvest the leylines. I must protect Kailon—even if it means going against Amas to do it."

Sonnen nodded. "I will fly you there myself. This has all happened under my eye, in my House."

Danil's throat burned with gratitude. He knew how such an offer went against the proud nature of the dragon prince. "Thank you," he managed.

"What about him?" Hafryn pointed with his chin at Griff. "He's not coming with us."

Sonnen grunted in agreement. "We must return him to Corros to face the consequences of his actions."

Danil held back a cry of dismay. They could scarcely afford to wait any longer. He'd already been gone from Kailon for too long.

"By all means, Sonnen," Griff replied, seeming to share similar thoughts. "Take your time."

Smirking, Griff didn't notice Patril stride up close from behind and slam her fingers hard against the nape his neck.

In an instant, his eyes rolled in the back of his head, and he slumped facedown into the dirt.

A moment of stunned silence fell about the camp as they all stared at the crow commander.

"That's quite a trick, Patril," Hafryn uttered, eyes wide.

"There are many ways to take a dragon down," Patril muttered nonchalantly, wiping her hand on her tunic. She turned to Sonnen and bowed. "My crows will take him someplace quiet and secure until your return, my prince."

Sonnen nodded his thanks, his expression a little nervous.

"Well, now that's settled," Hafryn said with a grin. "It's time we take Danil home."

28

The journey by dragon-wing over the mountains of Amas took three long, torturous days. Icy winds beat about Danil's cloak as he and Hafryn sat within the loose hold of Sonnen's talons. Danil found he hardly cared about the vista below as they flew over vast expanses of oak and pine forests, the land dotted with hundreds of small lakes and rivers. Instead, he clung to stubborn resolve that their return to Kailon would not be too late.

The leylines called to him with increasing urgency as if sensing his approach. Or perhaps it was Kaul's glyph they sensed. Even now, it burned so brightly that it was visible beneath the bandage. Danil had grown fearful of sleep, where visions of Kailon burning haunted his dreams.

But eventually they glided over the final peak, and Kailon came into view.

Held firm by Sonnen's talons, Danil squinted against the bracing wind to see a land once entirely made of blackened rock transformed by greenery. In his absence, new forests had spread through ravines, gullies, and canyons, and the rich scent of freshly turned soil hung in the air. Kailon was unrecognizable from only a few months past when Danil had been no more than a deadland scavenger risking his life for ancient relics and kiandrite flecks.

The forest came to an abrupt stop at the border of Roldaer. To Danil's dismay, he could easily see the ruins of Farin—someone had felled the sprawling trees and wiped the land clean of the wild new growth. Danil saw the red pennant of the Roldaerian magi affixed to the height of the crumbling inn.

Sonnen wheeled them over the Amasian camp.

To Danil's surprised relief, brightly colored tents still ranged the length of the gully. If he didn't know better, he'd have guessed that there were more tents now than when they'd left. "I thought everyone would be gone by now," he murmured dazedly.

Hafryn leaned close as shouts of welcome rang up from the camp. "Kailon's fate should be decided by those who care for it."

Danil looked at him sharply.

"Seems like the High Council has underestimated the resolve of Amasians," Hafryn said with a wry shrug.

They landed on a strip of exposed rock just outside the camp.

A sudden rush of dizziness overtook Danil as his feet landed amidst the rocks. The leylines clamored toward him, a loud cacophony of welcome and warmth that almost set Danil's heart at ease. The crystal against his chest thrummed a greeting in his mind, seeming to share images of their adventures and exploits with the leylines beneath them.

But then the glyph awakened with an all-too-familiar, sickening sensation. It pulsed, burning through the bandage until its ugly redness was exposed to daylight. Danil clenched his fist as the leylines grew hushed. The acrid taste of smoke lay thick on his tongue.

"Danil?" Elania gasped.

He glanced up to see Elania and Blutark hesitate on the edge of the rocks. Pennants bearing the House glyph of Corros furled in the breeze behind them.

Sonnen swept past Danil. "All is well," he promised the two enchanters, though his expression was strained. He motioned them all down to the camp.

Danil felt his attention drawn to the east. That way lay the Temple of Kaul. But was it the dreaded glyph that was calling him there, or something else?

Hafryn touched his elbow, offering both comfort and a steady presence.

"What would you have us do, custodian?" Elania asked into the quiet, noticing the direction of his gaze.

Danil glanced back at her. Her eyes were cautious but trusting. "I'm pretty sure this is a bad idea," he admitted.

Hafryn gave a huff. "That's hardly stopped us before, *fala*."

Blutark grunted in agreement. "We're with you, Danil. You should know the magi have felled the trees growing about Farin. Our spies say they've dug trenches around some of the buildings."

In alarm, Danil turned to Hafryn and said, "Arlyn must have sent word to Roldaer about the first crystal."

"And Farin will only hold their interest for so long," Hafryn warned.

Hoping he wasn't about to fall for some ancient plot left in place by Kaul, Danil hurried for the trail leading away from the camp. He felt the others follow close behind. The path took them through what could be mistaken for old growth forest, with huge pines affording little light down to the undergrowth, where only fungi and sporadic tufts of bracken fern grew.

As they loped, Hafryn quickly filled in Blutark and Elania on all that had happened since leaving Kailon, from kiandrite-sparked visions to Viren's betrayal and their eventual escape with the glyph burned into Danil's skin.

"Viren will not escape what he has done to both of you," Blutark promised, fingers twitching as if to weave an enchantment.

"I know of a hidden pass leading through the High Reaches," Elania piped up, her dimpled smile in sharp contrast to the murder in her eyes. "We can go together," she said to Blutark.

The bear shifter looked sorely tempted, and Danil was heartened by the way their Trueforms bared their teeth in agreement as they padded next to each other.

Hafryn chuckled. "I admire you each for your bloodthirstiness, but Danil and I get to decide my cousin's fate."

"Only if you reach him first," Sonnen rumbled.

Danil glanced back at his companions, feeling a rush of gratitude toward this unlikely gathering of friends. His only hope was that he was not leading them to some sort of dire trap. With each step, the glyph turned darker as if in hungry anticipation.

They trekked through a clearing bright with wildflowers before taking the path leading down into a grove where only patchy scrub grew amongst the exposed rocks.

To Danil's relief, the mine tunnel leading to Kaul's temple sat undisturbed, lined with the same shrubs he'd seen in his fiery vision. But in front of the entrance, where previously there had been only bare rock and thick boulders, sat a pool of tranquil water.

"Well, that's new," Elania muttered warily, coming to a halt before it.

Sharing a look with Hafryn, Danil trotted to the edge. The water was ice-cold and startlingly clear, revealing a wide fissure in the rock. Water could be seen burbling up from the deep, where a faint iridescent light resided.

Blutark squatted, his eyes narrow. "That looks like kiandrite," he muttered, gaze on the fissure.

"A new crystal?" Elania asked.

The water rippled, and Danil heard the leylines murmuring as if from only a few feet away. The first crystal gave a reverent trill, turning iridescent to match the glow within the fissure.

"It's the well," Danil realized softly. "It must have abandoned the temple." He glanced about, uncertain why it would have chosen here of all places to reside.

'*It's not safe,*' he sent out to it, together with an image of magi coming with shovels and curses to tap it dry. The well needed to go back deep into the earth, where it would be safe from Roldaer and perhaps even the glyph Danil carried.

Gentle laughter filled his mind as something new drifted out of the fissure. It settled on the surface of the pool, pushed along on a small wave until it fetched up against the rock at Danil's boots.

Bending, Danil fished out a sodden scrap of parchment. It threatened to fall apart in his hands, and he carefully unfolded it to see the charcoal markings within.

"Hafryn," Danil murmured, staring at the familiar spiked edges. He upturned his hand, where the same symbol pulsed a virulent red. "It's Kaul's glyph."

Hafryn took the fragile parchment, frowning. "It is, *fala*, but there are a few extra markings here. See?" On the edges of the drawing, five spirals softened the harshest lines. Hafryn tilted his head, his frown deepening as he scrutinized the parchment. "But I recognize this, also..."

Heart thundering, Danil recalled weeks before being gently guided by the leylines, the first crystal gripped tightly in his hand as he scrawled across a scrap of parchment. Glancing at his friends, he said grimly, "It's because I drew it the day the first crystal emerged. I drew Kaul's glyph."

THE BURNING GLYPH turned exultant on his palm. It scorched hot and bright, small new blisters starting to form.

Despite being dead for centuries, Kaul still held sway over the leylines he'd once imprisoned. It was the only conclusion Danil could reasonably draw. The dreaded halfbreed had somehow reached down through the ages and steered Danil's path.

"You said Kaul's magi-generals carried this glyph." Danil turned to Sonnen, numb. "What did they do with it?"

Sonnen's mouth thinned. "There are types of kiandrite that no one dares touch, Danil. In lands such as Amas, where all creatures live and eat and breed and die, kiandrite becomes absorbed into our very beings. Such kiandrite can be...released, through a violent death."

"Violent death," Danil repeated with a bitter whisper. "You mean like fire?"

Hafryn cursed softly in sudden understanding. "Your visions, *fala*."

Even now, Danil could taste smoke in the air. The leylines had tried to warn him—or prepare him for the inevitable.

"And Kaul's glyph?" Danil pressed, his heart a heavy beat in his chest.

Sonnen's expression was troubled and somber. "Even his magi-generals could not contain such evil. The glyph is a receptacle of sorts, designed to capture the death kiandrite until Kaul could take it and use it for himself."

Elania took Danil's arm in a gentle, comforting grip. "It's how the deadlands came into being, isn't it? Kaul used death kiandrite here and destroyed Kailon."

Sonnen nodded. "The ground may yet be tainted with Kaul's enchantments."

But Danil couldn't bring himself to believe that, not when the leylines were a bright presence seeking to gambol in the sunlight and fresh rivers and fertile soil. The pool rippled as if in agreement. It drew his attention back to the sodden parchment with its additional swirls and circles.

He waved the parchment into the air. "This glyph is different, though. And it was kept safe by the well itself."

Sonnen shook his head in warning. "I see your thinking, Danil. Altering the glyph you carry would be most unwise. We cannot know how these extra lines will affect the enchantment," he rumbled. "It may make it even more powerful."

The leylines whispered, trying to catch his attention.

"But—" Danil began.

"That Kaul's glyph has returned now, to ride upon the flesh of Kailon's first custodian." Sonnen shook his head, a deep rumble in his chest. "We cannot ignore the possibility that a remnant of Kaul yet remains here. You must face the possibility, Danil, that the leylines may be compromised."

A grumbling entered Danil's mind. Even his crystal turned a disagreeable yellow.

"The glyph has to go," Blutark muttered. "Sonnen, there

are enough enchanters back at the camp that we can attempt a cleansing. Only then can we turn our attention to freeing the leylines of Kaul's filth."

"A cleansing won't remove the glyph," Elania told Danil. "But it may quieten its effects."

Danil glanced at Hafryn to see him shrug. "I trust your judgment, *fala*."

Only a madman would want the glyph still on them. Danil lowered the parchment back into the water and nodded, though a nervous energy went through him.

Blutark took the lead, stalking to the end of the grove and beginning the walk up the embankment.

An enchanter met them at the top. She was sweaty and bleeding, eyes wild. Blutark steadied her with a grunt as she staggered.

"My prince," she gasped out. "Magi are attacking the camp."

Hafryn threw Danil a shocked glance. Above the tree line, a funnel of smoke rose up where the camp sat. Reaching out to the leylines, Danil sensed only grumbling discontent rather than alarm.

Sonnen glanced down at the glyph on Danil's palm and growled. "What do we face?" he asked the enchanter.

"Dozens. More are spreading out amongst the gullies," she panted. "There was one magus—she somehow knew the best path to reach the camp. Her party ignored us when we tried to lead them into the scree fields."

Twin flames gathered in Sonnen's eyes. "The magi cannot discover that the heart of the leylines resides beneath our feet. They must not reach this grove."

"We'd best hope you weren't followed," Hafryn told the enchanter.

She shook her head. "I was sent ahead when we realized they'd come to destroy the camp."

In the distance, the smoke turned an angry orange as more of the camp burned.

"Elania and Blutark, stay here with the custodian and Hafryn," Sonnen commanded. "I'll send more enchanters to defend the ridge." He pointed at Danil. "Do not use the glyph, Danil."

Mouth thinning, Danil nodded.

The dragon prince took the injured enchanter with him, both disappearing into the trees.

"Blutark and I'll stay up here," Elania muttered, eyeing the terrain. She motioned to Blutark to find a hiding place amidst a thick stand of bracken ferns. "You two stay out of sight in the grove." She studied them both and abruptly pulled Danil into a hug before similarly reeling Hafryn in. "Don't do anything stupid," she whispered to them.

Easing back, Hafryn gave her a jaunty wink. "No promises, Elania."

Snorting, she waved them off to find her own hiding place in the greenery.

Danil trotted down past the sparse vegetation to find a place behind a series of boulders set between the strange new pool and the mine entrance leading to Kaul's temple.

"Not ideal," Hafryn said as he settled in beside him. "But it'll have to do."

They waited in the quiet as smoke gradually drew closer.

A thick pall of it soon rolled into the grove. It stung their eyes. Danil reached out toward the leylines, and strangely sensed mournful regret and resolve. He peered around the boulder to the pool, but its surface was still.

Shadows moved in the tree line covering the ridge. Hafryn gripped his arm, motioning him to hunker down.

As many as ten magi sprinted along the ridge, their red robes a sharp contrast to the trees and verdant undergrowth. A heartbeat later, they struck up against an invisible barrier. Sparks and lightning shot across the ridge as Elania and Blutark wove their enchantments.

The magi responded in kind, with fireballs arching into the air to set the forest alight. Blutark made a quashing motion, smothering the nearest flames, as Elania released a new torrent of lightning.

Half the magi party broke away to skitter down the ridge.

Elania gave a roar of rage, fending off more fireballs but could do nothing as the breakaway party raced across the grove toward the pool.

The magi paused, grinning at the sight of iridescent kiandrite visible through the water.

'*Go down!*' Danil shouted to the well, begging it to disappear back down into the earth. The leylines shrugged him off.

Hafryn urgently gripped Danil's wrist, green eyes wide. "Look," he breathed,

Standing among the magi, and dressed in their matching red garb, was none other than Arlyn, emissary to the Kingdom of Roldaer.

29

W aving curtly, Emissary Arlyn directed the magi to fan out through the smoke-filled gully. She remained by the pool, casting a leery eye up at the ridge where Elania and Blutark still battled.

Behind her, one magus raised his hands, fire spewing forth to consume an evergreen shrub.

Peering cautiously around the boulder, Danil watched tortured flecks of kiandrite fly into the air like embers.

Another magus trailed after the first. He carried a plain silver box, the type folk used to store gems and semi-precious trinkets. Something about the box drew the kiandrite embers to it, where they disappeared inside with tortured pops and hisses.

"Death magic," Hafryn whispered, paling.

Danil could feel the leylines beneath them stir in anguish as more kiandrite was cruelly harvested.

"Hurry!" Arlyn ordered as she strode between the sparse vegetation. She stopped over a burrow, where Danil could sense pink-nosed moles cowering within. Arlyn muttered something under her breath. Fire exploded from her hands to funnel down into the hole, and tortured shrieks rang out. Flecks of red kiandrite drifted out of the burrow moments later.

"She's a magus," Danil gasped, guts churning in horror, his heart aching for the murdered creatures.

Hafryn's mouth thinned grimly. "Aye. And who knows what Amasian secrets she's garnered from within Corros."

Movement drew Danil's attention to the far edge of the gully. Another contingent of magi arrived, escorting a hooded woman in white robes trimmed with red. In the smoky haze, Danil caught sight of a dark braid lined with silver, then recognized the delicate profile of the woman's jaw as she turned about to gain her bearings.

"Magus Brianna," he breathed.

Hafryn shuffled behind the boulder to get a clearer view. He cursed. "Her memories were taken from her!"

Brianna grinned up at Elania and Blutark, who remained pinned in their fight on the ridge. Flaring her cloak about her, she turned around and pointed haughtily past the pool to the dark mine tunnel leading down to the temple.

Hafryn cursed once more. "We should have killed her when we had the chance," he snarled.

The heat began to grow stifling as Arlyn's magi continued to burn away the fragile life within the grove. Any moment now, they'd turn their attention to what lay beneath the water. Glancing about at the fire and smoke, Danil realized this was much like what he'd seen over and over again in his visions.

The leylines *had* tried to warn him.

Danil pushed to his feet.

"Wait!" Hafryn hissed, grabbing his sleeve and yanking him back down. "What are you doing?"

"I have to stop them, Hafryn! It's my duty as custodian!"

"How can you stop them?" Hafryn asked, gripping his shoulders tightly. His green eyes were frantic. "There are no enchanters down here, Danil."

"I don't *know,* Hafryn!" All he knew was that he'd promised to protect the leylines. He couldn't flinch when they most desperately needed him.

Hafryn shook his head angrily. "Not alone," he snarled. "You're not going out there alone and without a plan. That's a sure way to get yourself killed."

It stilled Danil for a few heartbeats, as the terror of Hafryn facing against magi and their flames set in.

"He has the right of it, *videre,*" a new voice agreed.

Whirling, Hafryn snarled and withdrew his blade. He slammed the newcomer against the boulder in an instant, sword at his throat.

Hands raised, Viren smirked. "Quite the welcome, cousin. I expected nothing less."

Hafryn released a wolfish snarl, teeth bared. "*You.*"

"Eloquent as always." Viren's smirk widened.

Danil suddenly noticed a huge owl perched upon the height of the boulder behind them. He recognized the blue-tipped wings and petulant gaze.

Merlias...

Other owls, larger and darker than any Danil thought possible, perched in silent vigil amongst the black rocks.

Viren set a finger against the hilt of the blade to nudge it back from where it scraped his throat.

Hafryn didn't move an inch except to bare more teeth.

Amusement in his green eyes, Viren slid his gaze to

Danil. "Call off your wolf, Danil. I'm here to fulfill our bargain."

Danil returned his gaze stonily. "Like you were going to do on the river?" he hissed. The yearning to *touch* Viren with Kaul's glyph suddenly gripped him.

"Just so." Viren smiled slightly. "You restored the glyphs of Eyrie as promised. Now I must ensure Hafryn lives. That was our agreement, yes?"

Danil stared at him as if he were daft. The roar of the flames grew more violent.

Viren's green eyes gleamed. "An Eyrie contract never goes unfulfilled, *videre*."

Hafryn pressed the blade closer until a thin line of blood showed on Viren's throat. "It'll end if you're dead, Viren."

The councilor had the audacity to shrug as a thick plume of acrid smoke rolled over them. "I see no one else coming to your aid." His gaze slid back to Danil. "Well, custodian?"

Even without looking, Danil could hear the crackle of burning vegetation draw closer. He nodded grimly. "I'll take it."

Hafryn gaped, his hard grip on the blade loosening slightly.

Viren took that moment to push the sword aside. Pulling a square of cloth from his pocket, he dabbed the blood from his throat. "Your plan, *videre*?"

Hardening his resolve, Danil muttered, "The magi can't take the pool or the tunnel."

"Very well." Viren's massive red Trueform trotted into view, fangs bared as the councilor signaled the waiting owls. "Lead the way."

Taking a final look at Hafryn's astonished face, Danil rose from behind the boulder. Through the smoke, he saw the magi were perhaps a hundred feet from the pool. Arlyn spied him from behind a wall of flames and gave a crow of delight.

Undeterred, Danil jumped over the ash-covered rock with a sense that destiny was upon him.

30

"Hello, Danil," Arlyn said, banking the fire slightly at his approach. "Come to re-join your people?"

The leylines clamored at him, their whisperings lost over the roar of the flames. Red kiandrite hung heavy in the air, whirling in the heat, but what caught his attention was the iridescent light he could somehow see in Arlyn's belly.

"You've ingested kiandrite," Danil realized.

Arlyn laughed in delighted surprise. "What a fascinating magus you'd make! I indeed had to purge all sign of mage-crystals from my body before entering Amas—an uncomfortable process, I assure you. But now that that game is played, I am free to be my true self."

Behind her, a magus pressed the silver box to the charred remains of a bush. Red kiandrite funneled into the box. Magus Brianna watched on with the other magi as if the collection of red kiandrite was necessary before they journeyed down to the temple of Kaul.

"Magus Brianna shouldn't recall this place," Danil said.

Arlyn tilted her head. "The curse mysteriously lifted

some days ago." She smiled brightly. "Most fortuitous, considering my success with the feckless Amasian council."

Danil wondered if the breaking of Brianna's enchantment coincided with his own unwilling acquisition of the glyph.

The whispering of the leylines suddenly urgent.

Hafryn trotted up beside him in his wolf form, bumping his shoulder against Danil's hip.

"Ah, your lover and—hello, Viren," Arlyn said, as footsteps sounded behind Danil. "Has your vote made you regretful already?"

Viren's green eyes were bright as he paused a few feet away. "Nothing I've done has been in your favor, Arlyn. You're not as clever as you think." He turned slightly. "She's stalling, custodian."

Danil could see that for himself. The magus with the silver box hurried amongst the burnt vegetation to harvest more of the death-tainted kiandrite.

Flames shot up to block Danil's path.

"You're already too late, traitor," Arlyn growled, her hand raised. "The legacy of Kaul Mage-kin is upon us."

Viren appeared amused. "Always on about Kaul, you magi," he tutted.

The Eyrie councilor raised his hand, and suddenly a handful of owls dropped down behind the curtain of fire. They moved with deadly precision, cutting up two magi before the Roldaerians could move. Arlyn whirled, the fire dropping low in her surprise.

It was Danil's best opportunity. Sprinting with Hafryn at his side, he leaped into the fray. Hafryn knocked over Arlyn with bared teeth and claws, but Danil had eyes on the magus with the strange silver box. Dagger in hand, he drove the magus away from the charred vegetation.

Viren must have shared his thoughts. A great red wolf barreled the magus over. Powerful jaws crunched down on the magus' throat, and the silver box went flying to smash open upon the rocks at the edge of the pool.

"No!" Arlyn cried.

A crystal tumbled out, blood-red and angry. Danil rushed to grab it.

The leylines shrieked in Danil's mind.

His fingertips barely brushed the crystal before Danil found himself...

...Somewhere else.

Thick smoke marred his vision. Danil coughed, lungs burning as he rose from his knees. A misshapen form emerged from the gloom, and Danil immediately recognized the horse-like body and blazing blue eyes. The Trueform shifted into a large man donning a black mantled helm and battle armor.

"Kaul," Danil managed.

"*Videre*," Kaul growled. His blue eyes were like ice. "You have prepared my lands well."

"Prepared—" Danil took a pace back. "Kailon isn't yours," he spat.

Kaul smiled. "Its leylines guided you to my glyph."

Danil clenched his fist. The glyph produced a steady heat. "You're wrong."

Kaul drew closer. "Let me show you its purpose."

The dreaded halfbreed was on him before Danil could lash out. Kaul slammed aside Danil's dagger with frightening ease and snatched up his wrist. Danil wrenched hard, but Kaul had him in an unbreakable grip.

Lip curling, Kaul used a taloned finger to trace the glyph on Danil's palm. It awoke with a deep boom, flaring to match the bright red crystal about Kaul's neck.

Danil struggled to jerk loose as Kaul yanked the red crystal free. With sudden ferocity, Kaul stabbed Danil's palm with the glowing red kiandrite.

Danil screamed, tripping backward to hit the ground hard.

The sound of battle suddenly rang about him.

Thick smoke roiled about him.

Hafryn was atop Arlyn, snapping and growling as the emissary fended him off with a dagger. Viren snarled, leaping over Danil to attack a magus attempting to build a wall of fire. The owls were spread through the grove, fighting more magi streaming down from the ridge.

Danil rolled in agony to find the red crystal still lodged in his flesh. The skin about the kiandrite quickly turned black. Dizzy, he shakily rose to his knees and hugged his injured hand close to his chest.

The leylines shrieked at him.

He glanced up to see a void form in front of him, tinged with red.

"Get back!" Viren roared. The owls took flight.

Arlyn rolled to her feet, bloodied and triumphant. "Ha! Fall to your knees, Amasians!" she cried. "Kaul Mage-kin has returned!"

Kaul stepped out of the void, wearing the very same battle armor as in the vision. A cloud of red kiandrite wrapped around him like a violent mantle.

"Dread lord!"

"Mage-kin!"

More shouts rang about the grove.

Danil scuttled back on his elbows, instinct driving him toward the pool. The leylines shouted at him, too fast and raging for him to discern the words.

Venomous blue eyes glowed from beneath the helm as

Kaul strode after him and dealt a tremendous kick that sent
Danil flying. Danil tumbled and skidded wildly, coming to a
stop at the edge of the pool. Blood flooded his mouth.

A dark shadow moved over him, and he blindly lashed
out. Another blow rocked him into the blackened stone.

"*Danil!*" Hafryn roared in terror.

A heavy knee forced Danil down. His eyesight cleared as
Kaul loomed over him.

"You have served me well, *videre*. I have one final task for
you." With a cruel sneer, the dread lord twisted the red
crystal free from Danil's hand.

Danil screamed, thrashing to get loose.

"Let us return this place to its true form." Kaul raised the
crystal with both hands over Danil's body, his face a rictus of
a snarl under the helm.

Hafryn barreled into the dread lord, knocking Kaul
sideways.

Danil rolled as the crystal slammed down where his
chest had been.

The crystal shattered like glass, spilling red kiandrite
across the rock. A fetid, rotten stench rose up as the ground
turned black and molten.

Kaul threw back his head and howled in fury at the loss
of his quarry.

Hafryn wheeled about to attack once again. Kaul easily
blocked the first blow with his arm guard, his eyes glowing.

"Move, *fala!*" Hafryn shouted as he danced away.

Danil scrabbled backward, all but tumbling into
the pool.

The well seemed to reach out to him, calling. Danil
glanced down to see that the fissure in the rock had blown
wide open, the kiandrite moving about as if in its own
current.

Danil snatched his injured hand away.

'*No,*' it chimed. It called to him once again.

Kaul must have heard. He brushed Hafryn off with a negligent blow and stalked to the water's edge. His gaze settled on the iridescent kiandrite. "What gift do you present to me now, *videre*?"

The liquid kiandrite trembled.

Danil gathered his feet and clenched his fists. "Kailon is not yours," he swore. "The leylines were never yours."

Smirking, Kaul stepped into the pool.

Hafryn, face bloody, skittered to a halt at the banks. "Danil! Run!"

A dragon's terrible roar vibrated the air, and then golden talons raked across Kaul's helm.

The dread lord's head snapped back from the force of the blow, and he bellowed his fury as Sonnen winged overhead.

From the corner of his eye, Danil saw Elania and Blutark race down the ridge with a handful of enchanters. They stopped at the edge of the blackening evilness. They threw glyphs at the ground to no avail as a terrible sickness clawed toward them, leaving a path of rot and death.

The molten blackness slithered across the grove. It consumed the last remnants of greenery, turning ferns, bracken, and budding seeds to ash. It grew stronger with every death. A handful of magi found themselves trapped amongst the jagged rocks as Kaul's poisonous enchantment roiled towards them. A magus fell screaming as the ravening blackness devoured her.

It's the deadlands all over again, Danil realized in horror.

Kaul threw his hands up and shouted unintelligible words. Molten earth shot skywards, and it took all of Sonnen's skill to evade the deadly projectiles. Hafryn staggered as the ground bucked and the black enchantment snaked toward him.

'*Custodian,*' the liquid kiandrite called.

Danil snapped his gaze to the water. The parchment floated to the surface and unfurled. The glyph, so like the one sitting damaged on his palm, took on an iridescent glow.

'*Complete the glyph.*'

He jolted, fearful of what such an undertaking would create. Already, the grove was falling under Kaul's power and death magic.

'*We will never be Kaul's,*' the kiandrite promised.

It was enough. It had to be.

Closing his eyes, Danil stretched his hand over the fissure and *pulled.*

The liquid kiandrite rose up to swell around him.

Kaul whirled. "What game do you play, *videre?*" he hissed.

With a forceful breath, Danil pushed his senses outwards, ranging across the dying grove and beyond. The kiandrite tumbled after him, spreading across ravines and scree fields, into undulating basins and quiet gullies yet to be burned. They spun together in a dervish of swirls and hard lines, and Danil heard the kiandrite laugh.

"What are you *doing?*" Kaul raged. He sloshed towards Danil, fists claw-like and reaching.

Danil opened his eyes. His injured palm knitted together, and the red glyph loosened to take on new lines and swirls. Danil raised his hand, feeling the truth and rightness of the reborn glyph as power surged through him.

Kaul took a step back in shock.

"Kailon is free of you, Kaul," Danil proclaimed. "And its

glyph, which you tried so hard to warp to your bidding, is lost to you. The House of Kailon is yours no more."

He drove his fist under the water to the hard rock below.

The House of Kailon awakened with a roar of light on the horizon. Its kiandrite blasted across the land, following a massive new path that matched the glyph radiating from Danil's palm.

The molten blackness exploded as iridescent light poured into the grove. The kiandrite pushed on, washing over the cowering magi as it swept over scorched earth.

Kaul shielded his eyes, howling as though in pain. The kiandrite slammed into him, toppling him head over feet out of the water. Verdant vines rapidly burst out of the ash, wrapping around his legs, chest, and arms where he lay. Kaul's hands became trapped at his sides, unable to so much as twitch to make an enchantment.

His glowing eyes raged from under the helm as more vines covered his mouth and jaw in a gag.

Its work done, the kiandrite seeped back into the ground with a gentle hum. Iridescent veins threaded through the rocks and boulders, showering soft light on the tiny budding ferns and plants now pushing up through the soil. A calm, contented quiet settled over the grove.

Rising, Danil gazed about in awe.

The kiandrite was a tinkling bell in the back of his mind. It rang out across the land, growing in potency until it became a thunderous declaration.

Kailon was finally free.

31

G reen eyes filled with wonder, Hafryn strode to the edge of the pool and offered Danil his hand. "This was your plan, *fala?*"

Danil barked a laugh as he splashed out of the water, the glyph on his palm emitting tranquil warmth. His crystal gave it a cheerful welcome.

The kiandrite all about them thrummed with contentment, save only for the veins tasked with containing Kaul. The dread lord was a malevolent force, murder in his eyes.

Danil resisted a shudder.

Hafryn hugged him close. "Let's not do this again, eh?" he whispered into Danil's neck.

Knowing how close they'd come to losing everything, Danil held on tight. "I'll do my best," he promised.

Elania and Blutark joined them, ash-smeared and weary but smiling nonetheless. Sonnen landed moments later, alighting with a powerful whomp of his wings. The air shimmered as he transformed, his face a mix of awe and relief. Kiandrite veins glittered as the last of the smoke dissipated.

"It is Kailon as it was always meant to be," Sonnen stated as he gazed about the grove. The dragon prince kneeled beside one vein, his expression reverent. "Forgive me for doubting you," he murmured, head bowed.

The kiandrite glowed an absolving blue.

Sonnen's gaze hardened as it swept to Kaul. "And you." He rose, stalking to where the dread lord lay bound. "I would leave you here to rot were it not an insult to have your foul bones remain in Kailon."

Kaul sneered. At Sonnen's request, the vines unwound themselves from Kaul's mouth but remained snug against his throat.

"I will not be contained for long, dragon," the dread lord snarled contemptuously, his eyes scheming.

Shouts drew their attention east, where the few surviving magi scattered up the ridge under the attack of Viren and his owls. They disappeared into the forest, where the magi's hollering turned to ardent screams.

Sonnen smiled thinly. "Your allies have already abandoned you, Kaul. I think you will find much has changed since you last walked in the world."

Kaul pushed against the entrapping vines but found no give. "I have lived beyond death. You would be wise to contemplate that before declaring your enmity, dragon."

Sonnen smiled again. "We will take our chances." He rose, dusting his hands on his breeches. He nodded to Danil. "When you are ready, custodian."

Stepping forward, Danil raised his hand. The House glyph brightened as if charged by the sun.

Kaul bared his teeth, thrashing. "There will be a reckoning, *videre!*"

Closing his eyes, Danil let the kiandrite guide the shape of the glyph. His fingers danced as the enchantment came into being. Beside him, Sonnen repeated the glyph, the gold of Corros intertwining with iridescent white. Then Elania and Blutark joined in, and the grove brightened to blinding.

The glyph wrapped around Kaul, weaving tighter and tighter until it was a blur. With a resounding crack, it hardened like stone.

Opening his eyes, Danil found the dread lord encased within clear quartz. Only Kaul's eyes moved within the chrysalis, promising death.

The kiandrite murmured in satisfaction.

"Stay with him until reinforcements arrive," Sonnen commanded Elania and Blutark. He smiled humorlessly. "Then I will help him discover a place so dark and deep that no magus may reach."

So long as it was far from Kailon, Danil was satisfied. His eyes tracked over the grove once more. A sapling as tall as his hip already sprouted beside the pool, its wide leaves extending toward the sun. More life stirred within the soil.

Hafryn came up beside him and bumped his shoulder. "Let's go home."

RAIN FELL upon Kailon as Danil, Hafryn, and Sonnen returned to the camp. The magi had fired their way through here, also, and destroyed all but a few of the tents. But veins of kiandrite spidered across the wet rocks bordering the path and boardwalks, and vast troves of the gully remained lush and green. A handful of shifters were already at work putting things to rights, collecting what items could be salvaged from the ash about the camp. To Danil's relief, many folk had managed to flee the camp unscathed, and as the day dragged on, they made their way back with stories of glittering kiandrite and a powerful glyph that had lit up the sky.

Helping Sonnen set up makeshift awnings, Danil realized with slow wonder that so many Amasians had defied the High Council and chosen to remain in Kailon. He turned to Sonnen. "You knew, didn't you? That the High Council was never going to give aid."

The dragon prince paused in his work to study him, golden eyes dimmed. "I had hoped to be wrong," he admitted.

"So why take me to Corros at all?" Danil pressed, frowning.

Sonnen lowered the rope he used to secure the awning. "Our people needed to see what Kailon had become." He smiled slightly. "And what you were capable of transforming it into. But it also gave Roldaer time to put their plan into motion, and for that I am sorry. Kaul's return was very much unexpected."

Danil swallowed, gaze turning east where the dread lord lay entombed and under guard. "Kaul knew about the House glyph," he murmured.

Sonnen nodded. "I suspect now that it had come into being the moment he brought the stolen kiandrite into Kailon. Kaul however, in his rage and hate for Amas, broke the magic so that the balance between life and death present in all House glyphs was destroyed."

Danil thought of the venomous red glyph that had burned through both his flesh and dreams. It had been the House glyph, stripped of all good intent so that all that remained was foul and twisted.

"It was never Kaul's objective to be a custodian," Sonnen

said, his thoughts clearly on the same trail. "But to heal a broken glyph, it must first be fully awakened."

"Which is how Kaul was able to come through," Danil surmised. He watched Hafryn work to clear the cooking area with a handful of other Amasians.

"Aye, but it would not have been possible without that cursed crystal," Sonnen rumbled, his expression troubled. "There are writings which speak of Kaul bearing a red first crystal."

Danil eyed the dragon prince's brooding face. "His relics keep finding their way into magi hands." He feared what may happen now that Kailon was luminous with kiandrite. The magi's hunger would only cause them to take even darker paths.

"That is something for me to rectify, custodian," Sonnen promised, flames in his eyes.

They returned to their task as light rain drizzled over the gully.

Sodden and dripping, Elania and Blutark arrived soon after with news that the few surviving magi had fled to Farin.

Hafryn trotted over, green eyes dark. "What of Arlyn and Brianna?"

Danil couldn't recall seeing them after Kaul had attempted to poison the land.

Elania hesitated. "There's been no sign of the emissary, but Magus Brianna is in Farin. The Eyrie have her. Viren has sworn to, as he put it, 'remedy things'." She visibly swallowed.

Eyes narrowing, Hafryn folded his arms. "While he's always been meticulous, Viren's not the type to overextend himself."

Danil wasn't fooled either. Clearing Farin of its magi

went beyond Viren's oath to Hafryn's safety. Still, Danil couldn't ignore his relief that Brianna would haunt him no more.

Blutark growled, "We can't assume that Arlyn died with the other magi in the grove, either. I'll organize a search party."

Sonnen nodded. "She saw Amas at its most fractured. We cannot let her use that against us." His gaze settled on Danil. "Kailon trusted that you would find a way to make the glyph whole again. The birth of your House has always been your path ever since you first lowered your hand into the temple well. You are under my protection as you continue to learn your way—Kailon will never stand alone."

The leylines released a low, contented hum in acknowledgment of the dragon prince's vow.

Dazed, Danil said, "I'm honored, Sonnen, and so very grateful. But how long can you defy the High Council?"

There had to be repercussions. While Kailon might stand outside of Amas, Corros certainly did not.

Sonnen smiled, baring sharpened eyeteeth. "Leave the High Council to me. Word of what has happened will spread across Amas, and I know my people. You have achieved everything the leylines have asked of you and more, Danil of Kailon. You are custodian and *videre*. Creator of balance in a land once known only for death. Protector of Kailon and Amas."

Hafryn huffed a soft laugh. "Geez, *fala*. Let us bear some of the weight."

Sonnen's smile widened. "And so we will," he promised.

32

The Eyrie returned as evening darkened the campsite. Viren disappeared with Sonnen into a makeshift tent to speak briefly but emerged soon after. The councilor strode with a purpose to the edge of the camp where Merlias and the other owls waited.

It took Danil a moment to realize Viren and the Eyrie were departing. He hurried after Viren and grabbed his arm. "You don't get to leave without explaining yourself," he hissed angrily.

Viren appeared startled but quickly became amused. He stepped away from the owls. "Whatever do you mean, Custodian Danil?"

Danil's eyes narrowed. "You knew what I was even before Freyna did." Even now, the councilor's wolf watched him with piercing intensity, as if trying to discern his secrets.

"Ah," Viren smiled. "It's true you're not the first *videre* to walk in Eyrie."

Danil studied the man's green eyes, so like Hafryn's in color. "You're referring to Kaul's *videre*."

Viren's smile widened in approval. "It was pure

assumption, of course, that another of her kind could undo the entrapment she'd wrought upon our glyphs. You understand I had to test it for myself."

Danil set his jaw, unable to shake his dislike of the man no matter how Viren had helped during the battle. "Were you really going to do it—kill Hafryn if I couldn't release your glyphs?"

The councilor seemed delighted by the question. "What do you believe, custodian?"

Danil glanced again at the massive wolf Trueform. It had stayed close to Hafryn in battle, fighting and protecting in turn. He gave Viren a narrow-eyed look. "I saw your wolf during the fight."

Viren's expression cooled. "Did you really, custodian?" he asked, voice deceptively mild.

Remembering the Eyrie's almost murderous obsession with keeping their Trueforms hidden, Danil's gaze slid past the councilor's shoulder to the waiting owls. Merlias' blue-tipped owl watched with steady intent. Noticing his stare, she clacked her beak in warning.

"Not everything you see is as it seems, Danil of Kailon," Viren said. "Every tide must turn."

A flash of irritation shot through Danil. "You're hardly the kind to speak in riddles, Viren."

The councilor's smile returned. "Then I shall speak plainly, custodian. The treaty is already broken, and when enchanters and other folk discover that the High Council put their own safety ahead of protecting our beloved kiandrite, there will be a reckoning."

Danil frowned. "And what—you'll be there to see it come to pass?"

His green eyes gleamed. "We are certainly not done with Roldaer. I know you see it, too."

Yes, Danil thought, knowing they were hardly ready. He glanced at his palm, where the new glyph shone bright and true. *But we will be.*

"When all is done, I may send aid your way," Viren said. "We share common interests, after all."

Viren surely meant Hafryn. In spite of all the man had done and the pain he'd inflicted, he still claimed a level of kinship with Hafryn that had seen him fight off a dread lord.

Danil searched Viren's face, wondering if he'd ever truly understand the depths of him.

The councilor of Eyrie gave an enigmatic smile and walked away.

GUIDED BY A LIT TORCH, Danil found Hafryn at the opposite end of the gully. He sat despondently upon a boulder overlooking the stream as it disappeared into the yawning dark of the mine shaft.

"Your cousin's gone," Danil murmured, climbing up beside him. Seams of kiandrite in the boulder combined with the torchlight to cast long shadows on Hafryn's face.

"Fair news at last," Hafryn muttered. He tossed a pebble into the stream.

As the silence stretched, Danil tried another tack. "Elania's sent word to Freyna. We should see more Amasians in Kailon in the next week or so—those who want to join the fight, that is."

In truth, he couldn't blame anyone for hesitating. The return of Kaul showed there were no depths the magi wouldn't sink to in their hunger for kiandrite.

Hafryn's gaze swept out over the stream but didn't comment.

"You have me worried," Danil said after some time, watching him. "I understand if you want to return to Corros. There's no safety or peace here. Not for long."

Hafryn finally turned to him gave him a wry smile. "After all we've been through, *fala,* a whole Roldaerian army isn't going to sway me."

It eased the heaviness in Danil's heart. "Then what's wrong?" he pressed.

Hafryn sighed and rolled up the loose sleeve of his tunic. The Eyrie House glyph on the inside of his elbow was faded to white, the magic within it spent.

Danil stared. "But—"

"I'm not Eyrie, *fala*. Haven't been for a long time, I guess." He smiled, bittersweet. "I suppose I didn't want to accept it before now." Sighing, he put his arm about Danil's shoulders.

Heart aching, Danil leaned in. "You're leaving your House."

Hafryn's mouth softened. "My path leads to another."

Another House, Hafryn meant. Danil knew because he bore its fledgling glyph on his skin. "Kailon might be the shortest-lived House in the history of Amas," he warned.

"Or the most glorious," Hafryn countered. He gave a rakish smile and planted a warm kiss on Danil's brow. "How can it not, with us at the helm?"

Danil managed a smile. "I know which ending I'll fight for."

Hafryn drew him close as Danil gazed out over the stream. An iridescent glow emanated from the pebbled bank, its changing whorls of color matched by the first crystal as it hummed contentedly in the back of his mind. A surge of responsibility gripped him. In this small pocket of Kailon was more kiandrite than he'd ever imagined possible when he was a deadland scavenger. And they'd come so close to losing it all.

But he would fight to protect this place, and all of Kailon. Even if it meant facing down powerful magi and dread lords whose malevolence stretched through the ages. Danil swore Kailon would never be subjugated again.

The glyph on his palm brightened with promise.

ABOUT THE AUTHOR

K K NESS is the pen name of identical twins living in Australia. They both share a love of characters whose antics make them happy, and enjoy competing against each other to see how much mayhem can happen in a story. They currently reside in sunny Queensland with various family and animal friends.

Visit their website for the latest releases and updates.

www.kkness.com

BEFORE YOU LEAVE...

Reviews are the lifeblood of authors. If you enjoyed Visioner (or even if you didn't), please leave a review on the way out. Your support and feedback is everything!

www.ingramcontent.com/pod-product-compliance
Lightning Source LLC
Chambersburg PA
CBHW030641110726
47901CB00002B/522